Go to work and do your job.
Care for your children.
Pay your bills.
Obey the law.
Buy products.

Praise for Noah Cicero

"I read Noah Cicero and remember that "hysterical" can refer to something really funny and to a situation completely out of control. His work punches people in the face. Don't get in its way."

—Daniel Handler, AKA Lemony Snicket

"It's full of angry, humorous and intelligent insights. I read it in one sitting."

—Harvey Pekar

"What is shocking about The Condemned is its confidence and sense of purpose. Really, really brilliant and readable."

—Ned Vizzini, author of *It's Kind of a Funny Story*

"I like your voice because you do not explain things that are obvious."

—Tao Lin, author of *Taipei*

Go to work and do your job.
Care for your children.
Pay your bills.
Obey the law.
Buy products.
by Noah Cicero

A Lazy Fascist Political Thriller

Lazy Fascist Press
an imprint of Eraserhead Press
205 NE Bryant Street
Portland, Oregon 97211

www.lazyfascistpress.com

ISBN: 978-1-62105-128-2

Edited by Cameron Pierce

The Interview

I was nervous. I was wearing a nice pair of slacks and a button-down, long-sleeved dress shirt with a tie. The tie looked great. I looked great. Everything seemed wonderful. I was a man interviewing to get a job working for the government, but I was nervous.

I walked up to the entrance and hit a buzzer. A man replied, "NEOTAP."

"My name is Michael Scipio," I said. "I'm here for an interview with Rachel Heidelberg."

The door clicked and I entered, only to find myself facing another door.

Now there was a door behind me and a door in front of me. A man stood in this space between the two doors. I looked at the man. He looked polite, slightly overweight, but still constructive and useful to society. He looked like he had never committed a crime, came from a good family, a family where no one went to jail, where people were educated and got jobs that required skill and hard work. He had lived a normal life, been properly educated. He was responsible. A responsible man doing a responsible job. I said to this man, "Can I enter?"

The man looked at me and said, "You cannot ask to go beyond that door."

"How do I get beyond that door if I cannot ask?"

"The door will open or it will not open, then you will go through it or you will not go through it. The door behind you is now locked. You can't go through the next door unless it opens."

"So I cannot ask to go through the next door."

"Correct."

"Then how do I get to my interview?"

"I am not allowed to answer any of your questions because you are not allowed to ask any questions."

The door clicked and I passed through it.

I entered another, bigger room.

There were two chairs and three doors here. A hallway led somewhere, but I did not know where the hallway led.

I walked up to one of the doors. It led to a room that was all windows. I told the people inside I was there for an interview.

A man came to the door. He looked to be in his mid-twenties. He didn't smile or frown. He didn't ask me who I was. He simply said, "Please wait. Take a seat."

So I sat down in one of the two chairs.

No one came into the big room. I was alone. There was no music, almost no sound at all.

Ten minutes must have passed before I heard a woman's clatter along the hallway, approaching me. She was a tall woman, mid-thirties, with long red hair.

She smiled at me. The smile was false. She was smiling because she considered it the thing to do when meeting someone. I smiled back. My smile was false. I was just trying to get a job.

She introduced herself as Rachel Heidelberg, and then gestured for me to follow her. We walked down the hallway to a small office.

She sat at a small roundtable beside a bald man who must have been close to her in age.

The man with the bald head introduced himself as Bruce Veits. He told me to sit down at the table with them.

They did not explain why Bruce was there or who he was. He was just there, staring at me.

I stared at them, Rachel and Bruce, waiting for the interview to begin. Both of them wore wedding rings.

"Tell me something about yourself," Rachel said.

They wanted me to tell them normal things, things that made me sound like a good, reliable employee. I had to make things up. I was applying to work in a prison/treatment center. The men and women in there were criminals. It occurred to me sitting there that I had partaken in many criminal acts.

I felt compelled to tell them about the terrible things I had done, but I knew that was a bad idea. I started to feel like trying to get to a job in corrections was a bad idea, but I needed a decent job, needed health care, needed to start rebuilding my life.

I responded, "I enjoy hiking in the forest. I've been to the Colorado Rockies National Park three times. I have hiked up several of the mountains in the park and found it a great challenge to get up those mountains. I love to do community service, like volunteer work. I've helped with community gardens and the Christmas festival downtown. I enjoy spending time with my family. Without my family, you know, life wouldn't be worth living. My family is very supportive of me and I am very supportive of them."

Later in the interview, Rachel asked me, "What do you think causes crime?"

I sat there, recalling what I had learned in sociology class. I said, "Crime is caused by a person who grows up in a situation where the value of obeying the law is not fostered. Commonly these are low income people who the law did not favor. The poor whites, blacks and Hispanics grow up thinking that the law is not for them because the law did not help them get what they wanted out of life, so they don't value the law because they perceive the law does not work for them. But there might be other reasons. They might be chemically imbalanced. And also there are economic reasons. Since America has lost its manufacturing base and the manufacturing jobs that remain do not pay well, the people of the lower class have fewer opportunities for decent-paying jobs, and since most of the jobs available to them hardly pay well enough to support their families, they do not receive any positive reinforcement from their employment. And some of them resort to crime."

"No, crime is a choice. Do you not believe that crime is a choice?" Rachel said. She sounded offended by my answer.

It occurred to me that maybe I had never thought seriously about crime.

I wanted the job, so I replied, "Yes, crime is a choice."

Rachel seemed pleased to hear this. She said, "Yes, crime is a choice. These criminals commit crimes because they choose to. We have to redirect their choices. Their choices are bad. Their choices and thoughts are incorrect. Society cannot tolerate their choices. They choose to commit crimes because they want to commit crimes. We must repress their criminal motivations. We must take their criminal thoughts and replace them with positive thoughts. Thoughts that lead to good things. Do you understand?"

I didn't understand a thing she said, but I nodded and told her I did.

"These are career criminals. They live to manipulate. They don't care about anyone but themselves. They don't care about you. They don't care about me. If they cared about people, they wouldn't have stolen from other people. They wouldn't have done drugs or neglected their child support. They will try to manipulate you in every way possible. They will try to get things from you. They will try to win you over so they can manipulate you. They have spent their lives complaining and crying like little babies. They are crybabies. They aren't men or women. They are children. This is what they have chosen. They choose to be children. We have to make them into adults. Do you understand what a career criminal is, Mike?"

"A person who manipulates and steals."

"Yes, and America needs good citizens."

"Yes, that's true."

"Good, then you agree with us."

"Of course."

I didn't know what I was agreeing with. According to her, people commit crimes because they want to commit crimes. They don't steal because they want an X-Box and can't afford it. They steal because they want to steal. They don't do drugs because they want to escape reality or repress something, but because they have such little regard for other people that it's criminal.

The interview was over.

I hoped I got the job.

I needed money.

I needed health care.

The Tour of the Building

Rachel Heidelberg brought me to another large, glass-walled office. Rachel showed me a giant computer screen displaying fifty images at a time, rotating every ten seconds or so, each image from a different security camera. There were cameras everywhere. Every inch of the facility was covered with cameras. Some of the cameras could even move with a click of the mouse.

"These cameras keep us safe," Rachel said. "These criminals can't do anything without us watching. We can see their every move and every employee's every move. I have a computer in my office. I can look at this at any time. I can also watch it from home. I can wake up at two in the morning and access these cameras. Everyone at NEOTAP knows they are being watched, but it works both ways. I'm being watched too. Surveillance is essential to a successful correctional institution. A surveillance system is pervasive like God. We have recreated God watching over us, judging us every second. The criminal cannot be left alone to behave how they want. They know the whole time they are being watched and judged and that they could receive a write-up, or WU as we call them. The surveillance system and the WU is our greatest weapon against the residents. We don't carry weapons, we don't carry mace or Tasers. The residents live in a constant state of fear and nakedness. They are naked before these cameras. They don't have their drugs, they don't have their women, they don't have anything. We have basically stripped them of everything they ever knew. They have no history, no identity in NEOTAP. We take away their ghetto or trailer park, we take away their ability to be a big-time drug dealer, we take away their talents. If they can play music, it doesn't matter here. If they depended on their mothers to supply them with money and love, well here, they get none of that. They don't get money or love or a mother. No one in here has parents. NEOTAP replaces God and parents. We have surveillance to replace God and we feed them and shelter them and direct their behaviors, replacing their parents. We don't allow any gang behavior in here. If we see two residents hanging out with each other for too long, we separate them. We don't want them to become friends. We don't want them to have conversations about drugs and women. We want them to have appropriate conversations. They need to live appropriate lives. We are guarding against all inappropriate ideas and thoughts that may arise inside their criminal minds. They are reborn here, they are like little fetuses, and we must raise these fetuses. Everything is gone. They are psychologically stripped naked before everyone. Do you understand the importance of surveillance in that process, Mike?"

"Yes."

"Do you have any questions about surveillance?"

"Yes—"

"Hold on, you can't ask any questions."

"Huh, I thought you said if I had any questions, I should ask them."

"You are only allowed to ask questions if I give you questions to ask."

"Are there any questions concerning surveillance that you think I should ask?"

"Yes."

I got extremely confused and didn't want to make her mad so I said, "Okay."

She replied, "Good."

It occurred to me while walking away that they could also watched employees. That I would also be watched constantly. That there was also a surveillance god watching me. That I wouldn't be able to play around or daydream or engage in anything fun while at work. I was going to be as paranoid as the residents.

I didn't understand why they called them "residents." They were trapped there, the doors were locked. If they escaped there would be a police hunt for them. Why didn't they call them "inmates" or "prisoners" or "convicts." They weren't "residents." A resident implies a person or even a plant or animal that lives in the same place for a long time, by choice. They weren't here by choice. They were placed here by the court system. They were closer to slaves or serfs than residents. They did not live in NEOTAP but were detained in NEOTAP.

Grownup Job

I called my parents and told them I got the job. They were excited for me. They told me to come over and they would get pizza and cake. My parents were very big into positive reinforcement. When I scored my first goal in soccer when I was seven, they bought me pizza and cake. When I was in the eighth grade talent show, playing guitar very badly, they bought me pizza and cake. When I got straight A's on my report card, I was for sure going to get pizza and cake. Pizza and cake are the ways Americans celebrate triumphs.

I drove into Deer Valley Estates. My parents lived in a beautiful suburban development. Which means I grew up in a suburban development. All the houses were relatively new and clean-looking. The yards were perfectly mowed and the hedges were trimmed. There was no crime except for teenage boy vandalism. There were no broken-down cars in the driveways, not a single shingle was missing. It was perfect. There was even a cul-de-sac.

I went into my parents' house. I had spent the last five years living in a dorm and then in an apartment right off campus, then recently, after college, I had moved in with my grandpa. Going back to my childhood home was not exciting to me. I walked into the house and it looked "nice." Everything in the house was ordered and clean and boring. We didn't live in an old country farmhouse or a mansion with paintings on the walls or spiral staircases. I really liked the old apartment I lived in by campus, with its old sinks and flaking paint. There was something human about it. You could tell that humans lived there. You couldn't tell that humans lived in my parents' house. They had the house remodeled once every five years. They would redo the kitchen and living room and bathroom, so people would think they were normal and up to date.

There were ceramic plates with pictures of horses on the walls and cabinets with strange teapots and figurines in them. My father was into photography. His nature pictures of hawks, the Grand Canyon, and bull moose running through the Rockies were all over the house.

My dad worked as a cameraman for a local television station. He stood behind a camera and filmed local news anchors for money. It provided good money and made him happy. My mother worked as a second grade teacher. It provided good money and made her happy. They had enough money to pay for things like remodeling their house, new cars, and vacations. They had worked the same jobs my whole life. They were determined people. They were determined to work the same jobs and be the same people from the day of my birth to the day they retired.

My father got up at four in the morning, put on his clothes and drove to work at the television studio. He had been waking up at four in the morning for so long that he didn't even set his alarm anymore. When my father got home he went straight to his bedroom and took a nap for an hour and a half and then got up to start his day. My mother woke at six, took a shower, put on her makeup, and drove to teach little kids cursive and times tables. When she got home, she would exercise on a treadmill for an hour and then cook dinner. After dinner, she would work on the next day's lesson plans. This routine was repeated every day.

My father had hobbies. He took a loan out five years ago and bought a sixty-thousand dollar camera to film movies and commercials for local businesses. He would go to a car lot and film a car lot owner wearing a cowboy hat or go to a lawyer's office and film a lawyer talk about disability insurance. Sometimes he would get to be on a movie crew. He especially enjoyed filming horror movies. The man loved horror movies and movies in general. Ever since I was little, whenever we watched a movie, he would tell me about the camera angles and the lighting. He would obsess over movies with bad camera angles and never stop talking about movies with good angles. My mother ran short marathons, not like twenty-eight mile marathons, but little five mile races for charity. She had won several events in her age class. She had a little shrine to the races she had won in the living room.

Sometimes I would think about their marriage. They had been married for twenty-eight years. They had my sister in their second year married and me in their fifth year. Then they stayed married while half their friends and family members got divorced. They stayed married and committed. Some years it seemed like they loved each other and some years I don't remember them even speaking to each other, but time passed and they would love again. There was a year when my mother got terribly depressed and wouldn't leave the house, but my dad said nothing, then one day my mom went to a counselor and she started exercising and doing marathons. About five years ago my dad had a small thing of cancer on the back of his neck, but they were able to fix it. I remember my mother crying a lot then. When my sister and I were little, we would take family vacations to Disney World and the Colorado Rockies, but when my sister and I hit our teens, family vacations ended. My father would go to a national park out west and take pictures and my mother would go to Spain, England or France for five days with her friend Donna. My mother loved Europe and couldn't get enough of it. She would sit and read books on European castles and their kings and queens. My father cared nothing for Europe. He didn't like cities or even the suburbs, but he knew he had to live there to have a job and maintain his family. Their marriage was full of compromises. I never knew when these decisions were made about vacations or about my mother's depression. I always assumed they took place at night when they were alone in bed, hiding away from their children. They never discussed their life plans with me. I had to discuss my life plans with them, but they were not obligated to discuss them with me.

When I came in my mother was wiping down the kitchen counters and she said, "Mike, you have a job. Give me a hug."

I gave my mother a hug. I felt nothing. I don't know why I felt nothing. We were never close, I don't think we ever had one real conversation our whole lives. We had lived together for eighteen years and I had known her for twenty-three years. The conversation was always the same. She would ask me about my life, she would tell me positive things, and she would tell me about the accomplishments of my relatives and kids from the suburban housing development.

We never discussed movies or how we felt about politics. The conversation was always determined by her and what she thought was important to talk about.

She said, "This is so exciting, your first grownup job!"

I looked at the kitchen table, where there sat a pizza box and a cake with the words 'Grownup Job' in frosting.

Then she started, "Is grandpa all right? Are you taking care of him?"

"Yes."

"Are you washing the dishes on time?"

"Yes."

"Are you taking the garbage out every week?"

"Yes."

"But you aren't treating him like a child, right?"

"No, I'm not treating him like a child."

"But you can't let him just do things. He is old and needs to be taken care of," said my mother.

"Yes, I know."

"What temperature do you have the house at?"

"I have it set for sixty-eight."

"Oh no, you need it to be at seventy. Your grandfather will be cold."

"It seems pretty warm in there," I said.

"No, that isn't warm enough."

"I think I know when something is warm."

"Are you eating right?"

"Yes, I have been eating a lot of salads and spinach."

"Spinach? You eat spinach now?"

"Yes Mom, I eat spinach now."

"You never ate spinach when you were little."

"I'm trying to eat healthier. I even started taking a flaxseed supplement."

"What the hell is flaxseed? Why don't you take a multivitamin?"

"Because multivitamins don't contain flaxseed," I said.

"How much are they are paying you?"

"$11.30."

"How are you going to get married and start a family with that?"

"I put out like forty applications. They were the only place hiring."

"Did you try your cousin Tony? He's got a political science degree and does the government contracts for constructions companies. Did you try him?"

"Yes, Tony said they aren't hiring."

"I thought you wanted to become a political consultant. Did you try the local consulting companies?"

"Yes, they aren't hiring either."

"What about the local non-profits, are they hiring?"

"I called all of them and none of them are hiring a political science major. They want like geologists and chemists."

"Oh, why didn't you just become a nurse like your sister? She makes twenty-four dollars an hour and put a down payment on a house, and did you hear about your cousin Carrie? She has an accounting degree and just got a big time job making fifty-thousand a year to start. Oh, why did you choose political science?"

"I don't know. I get the best grades in it. Shouldn't you do what you get the best grades in?"

"No, you should do what makes money. I became a second grade school teacher because that was a good job for a woman back then and I was able to pass the classes. With that job I was able to raise two children and pay off a home."

Then my father came in the room. I looked at him. I could see my nose on his face, my forehead and my mouth, all on his face. I couldn't look into the mirror without seeing that man staring at me.

Like a good Italian he walked over to the pizza, picked out a corner piece and started eating, and said, "Michael."

I didn't want to hear what he had to say. I said, "Yes."

"You really want to do this job, I mean I've never heard you mention wanting to work in corrections before. You are really nice, a bit too nice in my opinion. I don't think we raised you to be a person who yells at prisoners all day. I remember that one time we were in the city you saw that homeless black woman standing in the snow with those open-toed shoes on. You made me stop the car, then you took your sister's gym shoes from the backseat and gave them to her. And how you went to all those volunteer events in college helping poor people get food and Christmas presents. You're really friendly. This isn't really a job for friendly people."

I sat there wanting to leave and said, "I don't know what else to do. They were the only people that wanted to hire me. And like, the job is helping people. They told me in the interview that it was a treatment center, not a jail."

My father said in a firm voice, "Sounds like a jail to me. They are locked in there, right?"

"Yeah."

"Well that's a jail, not a treatment center. They might be giving them treatment, but it is inside a jail."

"I don't have to carry mace or any weapons, we don't have riot gear."

"Yeah, but my job has led me to meeting a lot of cops and people in corrections. Those people are all power hungry nutballs."

I sat there confused. Maybe he was right. I didn't know what I was getting myself into. I had never known anyone who worked in corrections. I wasn't even friends with criminal justice majors in college.

My father ate another piece of pizza and said, "See, I like my job. I like cameras, I like talking about cameras, I like getting new cameras, I like thinking about cameras, and camera angles. I love cameras. I don't even care about the local news. The local news can screw itself for all I care. I wouldn't mind filming birds or action movies, it doesn't matter as long as I'm surrounded by cameras and other people who love cameras. But I have never heard you express any love for corrections or criminals."

"But I've been told if I do this job for a year it will be a great reference."

"A great reference to what, being a cop?"

I sat there defeated. I didn't want him to talk anymore.

Then my mother said, "What happened to that girl you were dating in college? Linda?"

"Linda went to law school."

Then my father said, "Why don't you go to law school?"

"There are enough lawyers. The world doesn't need another one."

"But how are you going to make enough money to raise a family," said my mother.

"I don't know. The economy is really bad. What do you want me to do?"

"We want you to have a good job," said my father.

It had never occurred to me that I was supposed to have a good job. I still had no kids and no wife, which to me meant I had no reason to care about such things. I just wanted to have enough money to live and party a little.

My father said, "I think you were screwing around your senior year of college and didn't take the GRE or LSAT, and now you have to work this shitty job."

It was true; all I wanted to do was graduate and get on with my life. Everyone was talking about going to grad school or moving to Chicago or New York City to start incredible careers, but instead I would smoke weed and drink a few beers and go to sleep. People would ask me what I wanted to do after I graduated and I would tell them that I just wanted to start my life. It was true, I was tired of school. I was tired of showing up to class and listening to lectures, I was tired of doing assignments, I was tired of going to school all week and working on the weekends. I wanted days off, I wanted two days off a week to lay around and read a book, watch YouTube videos, and maybe get good at golf.

To keep them quiet, I said, "How about I take the GRE and LSAT this winter and apply for grad schools in the spring?"

My father nodded his head in approval and then my mother said, "You better start working on your math now. You know you aren't good at math."

"Yes, I will start working on my math."

I eventually left my parents' house. It was the same thing every time; all they wanted to do was discuss my life. My life was a huge issue to them. We never discussed their lives. According to them their lives were great. I believed it was a political stance that parents took, a nice, noble lie parents from the middle-class told their children. They told their children their lives were great and that if they did what they were told then everything would turn out great. I didn't know anything about my parents; they never discussed their personal feelings or childhood memories with me. I had no idea if my father was a drunk during his college years or if my mother was a slut in high school. I didn't know if my parents ever had suicidal thoughts or what kind of women my dad was attracted to. My parents had sex, but what kind of sex, I didn't know. As you grow older, you start to realize that your parents have lives of their own, separate from you, but by that time your parents have formed the habit of keeping you out of their lives, and no matter how old you get they will never let you get to really know them.

On my way home I wondered if my father was right. Was I making a good decision about working for NEOTAP? I knew it wasn't my dream job but I still hadn't figured out what my dream job would be. I had applied for jobs I actually wanted but they weren't hiring. It was either work for NEOTAP or work for a factory for $8.50 an hour or keep serving at a restaurant.

The Slogans of NEOTAP

Heidelberg led me to her office. To get to the office we had to walk through an area where the residents were sitting. There were about fifty residents in the room. I looked at them, some of them looked at me. They were career criminals. These people were considered so heinous and deviant that they needed to be locked up. The United States court system found that they could not control themselves, they were a danger to themselves and to others. Society deemed it necessary that large amounts of money should be spent locking them in a single building.

The room was silent.

Fifty career criminals and no one was talking.

Not a single mouth making a noise.

They were pacified. Sedated.

I said to Rachel, "No one is talking."

She responded, "Yes, isn't it wonderful?"

I said, "Yeah, it is great. So what does NEOTAP stand for?"

She said, "It's an acronym."

I read her face and it said not to ask any more questions, so I didn't.

The residents were allowed to wear any clothes they wanted. Almost all of them wore the same Nike shoes, jeans and baggy t-shirts. Their bodies looked strong. Many were widely built.

I asked Rachel, "Are they allowed to work out or play basketball?"

"They are allowed to do pushups and sit-ups after dinner. But residents don't come here to work out. They come here to be reformed. That was a correct question."

I knew then, I had to guess the questions. There were questions I was allowed to ask, but I had to figure out which ones I could ask. I could not ask what NEOTAP meant, but I could ask if they exercised.

I asked Rachel, "What is the recidivism rate here?"

"A lot of people ask that," she said.

I realized I could not ask that question.

Rachel led me into her office. There were barely any decorations except for Kansas City Chiefs memorabilia. There were a few pictures of her husband and children. On the wall in giant bold letters were the slogans of NEOTAP.

We sat down across from each other.

She said, "You look nervous."

"I'm okay."

Rachel smiled and said, "Do you like football?"

"I don't watch it much."

"I like the Kansas City Chiefs. Do you play fantasy football?"

"No."

"Oh, we all play fantasy football here. We are all in a league together. I have a pretty good team this year."

"That sounds good."

She stopped smiling and pointed to slogans written on

a giant piece of paper and said, "Do you see the slogans?"

"Yes."

"Those are the slogans of NEOTAP."

"Yes."

She handed me a piece of paper with the slogans on them. I looked down at the piece of paper. It was titled "The Slogans of NEOTAP."

She said the first slogan aloud. "If men were angels, we would not need procedure."

She went on. "This slogan means that men are not good. There is always a section of society that disobeys the laws. This section of society must be restrained from hurting themselves and other people. Society cannot stand law breakers. We have laws for a reason: to maintain order and peace. The law exists so people can live, go to work and raise a family. The law sustains us, but there are people who are greedy, selfish and manipulative, who do not value the law. These citizens must be restrained and reformed. If a citizen cannot be reformed then they will be sent to prison for the rest of their lives. Procedure enables us to live. Through procedure we know how to behave. To live a good life, a good American life, we must obey the procedures that guide our lives. There is a procedure for shopping at a store. You go in, you pick things out and then you pay for them. There is a procedure for voting. You register to vote, you find out where your voting station is, you go there, you wait in line politely and vote when notified. And just like life, there are procedures here at NEOTAP. Everything must be documented at NEOTAP. For a person to leave the building, five papers must be signed and a computer log must be filed. Everything here is documented in a certain way, everything here is procedure. These procedures are just, they coincide with the law. The law gives us direction on how to behave and how to form procedures. Do you understand?"

I replied, "Yes."

"The next slogan is 'Efficiency is the path to enlightenment.' This means that to be a good citizen one must believe in efficiency. Being efficient means you show up on time, it means you do your job, it means you follow the rules, it means that you don't make excuses, it means that when your boss tells you to do something, you do it. You don't ask why, you just do it. For things to run smoothly, things must be efficient. Society wants efficiency. It wants people who show up on time, do their job, do what they are told, and believe that what they are doing matters. These deviant criminals must come to terms that to survive they must become efficient. That society demands efficiency, here at NEOTAP we teach them to be efficient. When they become efficient they will get jobs, they will show up to work and do their jobs, they will get raises, they will pay their child support, they will pay bills, they will buy things and contribute to the consumer economy. By participating in the consumer economy their lives will be enriched. They will find happiness in work and buying products. Work will make them happy. Buying products will make them happy. They will have reached enlightenment."

She went on to the next one. I could see that she was enjoying herself. "'Repress criminal thoughts, submit to the law.' This means that criminals have criminal thoughts and we at NEOTAP teach them to repress those thoughts. We teach them what those criminal thoughts are and how to repress them. Their criminal thoughts will never go away, but at least we can get them to repress them and hate them.

The criminals must learn that submission is key to surviving in this world. The world demands submission to the law. The law is what keeps us safe. It is what keeps us strong as a nation. The law allows for happiness. If there is no law, then there is no happiness. The government supplies us with the law and they have weapons to back the law. These criminals must understand that they are not the law. We are the law, NEOTAP is a direct representation of the law. The criminals believe that they know better than the law, but they do not. They will never win against the law. The law is stronger and more powerful than humanity. The law is beyond humanity. The criminals must understand who is in control and what is the truth. The truth is the law. I love the law. I believe in it, I submit to it. The residents must also submit to it. If I have to submit to it, then they have to submit to it. Do you understand, Michael?"

"Yes."

She went on with another slogan. "'All deviants are guilty.' This means that everyone in NEOTAP is guilty when they are here. A court has proven that everyone here is guilty. Every time they do something wrong, they are guilty. If they get seven meatballs instead of six, even if it was an accident, they are guilty, they will be written up. There are no excuses for getting seven meatballs. If they have three magazines in their locker instead of two, they are written up, even if they have a good excuse. They are guilty no matter what. They are deviants and deviants are guilty. Do not ever ask them for an excuse. Do not ever allow them to have a reason or a cause or an alibi. They don't have one, they will never have one. You do not need to concern yourself with their reasons. They have no reason. If they had the ability to reason, they wouldn't be here. They are guilty because they are deviants and all deviants are guilty because they are deviants."

"The final slogan of NEOTAP is 'For the government so loved its citizens that it gave them NEOTAP. Only through responsibility may we gain happiness.' This basically means that the government loves its citizens and wants to give citizens a chance even if they are deviants. The government has decided to fund NEOTAP. The residents must understand that the government loves them. That the government is the law. That they should love the law because the government loves them. And if they submit to and love the law, they will, in turn, love the government. The government wants to reform these criminals into responsible individuals. Through responsibility these deviants may come to know happiness. Happiness is responsibility. Responsibility is efficiency. By going to work, by doing your job, by paying your bills, by paying your taxes, and taking care of your children, then you may learn what happiness is. We must teach them that happiness is not drugs, even if drugs make them very happy. Happiness is going to work for a company. Happiness is loving that company. Happiness is going to the mall and buying products with money you've earned by working for a company. Happiness is buying a large flat screen television and watching football on it. Happiness is going to work and making money and buying new clothes with that money. Happiness is paying bills. Happiness is paying off your debt. These things are what make a person happy. Drugs and crime do not make a person happy. The law does not want that. We must obey the law. Responsibility and efficiency are the keys to living a happy life in modern society. Do you believe that?"

I said without pause, "Yes, I believe that."

"You do not believe that religion can help these people? You do not believe that Freudian psychology or healing through the arts can help these people?"

"No."

"Good, but you must understand something. In your interview you stated a very sociological view of why crime exists, which might be true. But we are not concerned with truth here. Truth will not help these criminals. These criminals have no interest in truth. They have no interest in discussing ideas about truth or ideas about psychology. They don't care. They will never care. Most of them haven't graduated high school or only have their GED. They don't care about truth. We must accept that. They do not want truth. We must accept that also. They are interested in getting money and surviving so they can play video games and wear Nike shoes. And hopefully we can reform them enough so they want to at least pay their child support and go to work. This is our only hope, that we get them to go to work, hold a job, pay their bills and pay their child support. They are a drain on the system but since many do not commit crimes bad enough, we cannot lock them away forever. They commit only minor crimes, which require small sentences over and over and over again. While they are out for six months or a year they get women pregnant. These women don't care who the father is. They don't care about money to raise the children, they don't care about raising the kids to become adults. They don't care whatsoever about their children. The men only have children because it makes them feel like adults. They are truly worthless people but they still feel the need to procreate and have children. These children are a drain on the system. The government spends millions every year to take care of these children and their useless mothers. Their fathers are in prison or out committing crimes and do not care at all about what happens to their children. But the law states we cannot sterilize the criminals. We cannot even tell them to have fewer babies. We are not allowed to mention the fact that they recklessly have babies. We have forty women in the female ward, and most of them have children. Many are here for child endangerment. They don't care. You must understand that they don't care. They have different values than you. They don't believe that child rearing is an activity for responsible hardworking people who make enough money to raise children safely and in a good home. These ideas are alien to them, truth is alien to them. If they had any interest in the truth they wouldn't procreate. The job of NEOTAP is not to teach them truth or to be interested in truth. Our job is reform criminals into responsible, efficient citizens who go to work, buy goods and pay their taxes. Do you understand?"

"Yes."

"Do you believe in NEOTAP?"

"Yes."

"Correct."

I looked at the poster board and read the slogans again:

If men were angels, we would not need procedure.

Efficiency is the path to enlightenment.

Repress criminal thoughts, submit to the law.

All deviants are guilty.

For the government so loved its citizens that it gave them NEOTAP.

Only through responsibility may we gain happiness.

Over the Counter Medication

I was taken to a small office. In the office was an Arab man who was small and weak-looking. If any of these criminals wanted to bash his head in, Imad would have had no chance in the fight. He didn't smile as he held out his hand and introduced himself. "I'm Imad. I'm the second in charge here concerning your position. Second in charge, okay?"

I shook his hand and said, "Yes."

He handed me a piece of paper that showed the complete hierarchy of NEOTAP. It looked like a strange family tree. At the top was a man named Edward Choffin and then under him was a man named Robert Jones. He pointed to where he was on the tree and showed me where I was. He said, "You must remember hierarchy trumps procedure. If you are following a procedure and a person higher on this tree says to do something else, you do it. You cannot question it. You cannot reply that you are following procedure. You are currently at the bottom of this tree. Since you are at the bottom of this tree, you cannot question anyone above you. You cannot ask anyone else a question because they are all higher than you on the tree and they are not expected to answer any of your questions. You cannot answer any questions the residents ask you. They are lower than you on the tree. You are above them. Therefore you don't ask residents questions and they cannot ask you questions. You cannot ask anyone above you a question and you cannot ask anyone below you a question. No one above you will ask you a question because you are below them. Do you understand?"

"Yes. But how do I know what to do?"

"There will be memos."

"Where do the memos come from?"

"The memos will be in your mailbox when you get to work. The memo will be there, you will read the memo, and you will know what to do from the memo."

"Who makes the memos?"

"You cannot ask that."

"Oh, okay, sorry."

"Now we must learn about over the counter medications. An over the counter medication is like Tums. Do you know what Tums are?"

"Yes, a thing for heartburn."

"Yes, Tums are for heartburn. Every day we give the residents Tums. If they want Tums, they come to the counter and we give them Tums. We sign three pieces of paper recording who gets Tums. It is very important that we watch them eat the Tums. They must chew all the Tums in front of us. It takes a long time for the Tums to be passed out. If we do not watch them, they might not eat the Tums. They might go back to their room with the Tums and sell the Tums for food at lunch, commit suicide with the Tums, or even build a weapon and attack someone with Tums. Everyone in here has a criminal mind. They cannot be trusted with Tums. Every time you give them anything, they will take it and try to find bad things to do with it. We cannot allow them to do bad things. We must fill their heads full of positive thoughts. We want positive, good citizens that eat their Tums. We will not stand for weapons made out of Tums. They could take the Tums and make a key out of it, then use the key to open the doors and get out of the building. Then we have escape issues. We have to call the police, the police come, then the media comes. The media tells everyone that a criminal has escaped using Tums. Then the politicians in the capitol refuse to fund our facility because people escaped using Tums. Then you are fired because you didn't follow the Tums procedure. Do you understand?"

"Yes."

"I am glad you understand. Do you like fantasy football?"

"I've never played."

"My favorite football team is the Miami Dolphins. I think we can win some games this year. Our offense looks really good. I think we have a chance to get to the playoffs. I'm worried about my fantasy football team though, it doesn't look good. I didn't get a good draft."

I stared at him.

Imad and I left the office and went to something called The Watchtower. It was a little area with a counter and mailboxes for the residents. It overlooked the lower floor where the residents worked on assignments the cognitive behavioral therapy teachers gave them.

Imad sat down in a chair and said, "You can't sit around on this job. You have to keep busy. There are always things to do. You can't sit around and daydream, you have to stay alert. These are career criminals. These people are going to try to manipulate you every minute of the day. You must never give them a reason for why you are doing something. It is not required of us to give them reasons. We can tell them to clean the floor with a toothbrush, we can tell them to sit next to a wall alone for a week. We don't need to supply them with a reason."

Imad pointed to a guy sitting next to a wall. The man was in his twenties and looked like he hadn't combed his hair in weeks. Imad pointed and said, "That's Nick Pio. We stuck him on the wall a week ago. He isn't allowed to speak to anyone. He isn't allowed to do anything but work on his anger management assignments and read if he wants to. But he can't read very well, so he doesn't. He is allowed once an hour for three minutes to go to the bathroom. We have never told him why he is on the wall. We don't have to. We are in a position of authority. Authority is not required to supply reasons for their behavior, because hierarchy trumps procedure."

"Is there a reason for him being there?" I said.

"There was a memo to put him on the wall, so we put him on the wall."

"What was the reasoning on the memo?"

"The memo didn't state."

"Okay."

"This job is crazy busy. You have to stay busy."

Imad had been sitting in a cushioned seat not doing anything for ten minutes.

I eventually sat in the other cushioned seat.

Twenty minutes passed. We had not moved.

Thirty minutes passed. We had not moved.

The whole time Imad sat there staring. Sometimes he would talk about the Dolphins and how he thought they would have a good season. I wanted to ask him what nationality he was from the Arab world. I had read several books of history on the Arab, Persian and Turkish people and thought it might be interesting to discuss it with him. But it dawned on me he would never want to talk about his life with me. I was below him. I could not ask him questions.

Imad finally stirred after forty minutes. He said, "But before I call up the residents, this is the first time you will have interaction with the residents. You cannot have conversations with them. They are going to try to manipulate you. They know you are a new hire and they will try to take advantage of you every way they can. There is a target on your head right now. It says 'New hire, manipulate me.' You cannot talk to the residents. If they have a question, direct them to me. If you have a question while they are around, do not ask it. They cannot see if you have any questions. There are no questions while they are around. If one tries talking to you, no matter what it is, tell them to ask me. Even if they don't have a question, tell them to ask me. If they talk about negative things, we write them on the log. They know this. We know this. Everything they say must be positive. They must talk about how they will get jobs and pay their child support and not steal."

"But won't that lead to them just coming up to us and saying positive things so you will write that they said something positive in the log?"

Imad looked at me angrily and said, "No."

"Okay."

Imad called to the lower floor to get the fifteen residents to come up.

Fifteen residents came up.

It was my first real interaction with the residents.

They stood in a polite line not talking. There was some whispering but it was barely audible.

Each resident came up one at a time.

Imad checked a sheet, then signed another sheet and then filled out a large document concerning who took the Tums, how many they took, when they took them, and then he signed that one.

One came up. Imad filled out all the forms which took a minute, then put the Tums in a small plastic cup, then dumped the Tums into the resident's left hand. The resident put the Tums in his mouth, held up his left hand so Imad could see. Imad stared at the resident's left hand. Then the resident was required to chew the Tums loudly standing in front of him. When the resident was done chewing the Tums he had to open his mouth to show that he had chewed them to a point that he could not make a weapon or key out of the Tums. Then Imad would say, "You can go."

After it was over, Imad collected all the documents and put them into a special place. Then he went on the computer and filled out a log of everyone who took Tums and how many they took. The whole process lasted one hour.

Reality Conversion

Rachel Heidelberg led me to a small room. The room had no windows. There were no pictures on the walls. It occurred to me that nowhere in the building were there pictures. Everything was white, grey and blue. There were no other colors. The building was efficient. Everything was where it was supposed to be. There was no artistry, nothing inspiring about it. Rachel Heidelberg motioned for me to sit down. She looked at me and handed me a book called *Reality Conversion*. She said, "This book is our bible here. We believe in this book. This book notifies us of how we should think and behave and how the residents should think and behave. Everyone who works here believes in this book. *Reality Conversion* supplies us with a form for our program. It is important to become acquainted with it. Personally I do not like to read and find it boring, but I force myself to read this book once a year. The book was written by Dr. Charles Nevitsky. I personally don't know anything about the man, but I do believe his book. Now sit in this room and read for several hours. When it is time for you leave the room, I will come and get you. There is a camera in the room if you did not know."

She handed the book to me. I held it in my hands, looking at it.

Rachel Heidelberg walked out of the room.

I sat in the small room alone. I looked at the camera, then I looked back at the book and began reading excerpts from Dr. Nevitsky's *Reality Conversion*:

The Human Body and Its Mind

The human mind is nothing. The human being is a body. A body that must be fed, clothed and sheltered. The body knows that it must be fed, clothed and sheltered. In reality this is all the human body needs. The human body lives in a society. A society is a collection of human bodies, each body requiring food, clothes and shelter. Most humans in modern society decide to be normal and do work, which is finding a place in the society that contributes to the continuance of that society. The social contract of any society begins with the body; each body contracts with other bodies to fulfill their basic needs. We must recognize that man is a body and through the body there are behaviors. Behaviors are choices the body makes. Concerning deviants we must teach them how to make their bodies move into certain patterns. The deviant has a mind that creates thoughts, but those thoughts are not good thoughts. A human is a mass collection of thoughts. Statistically the criminal thinks bad thoughts more than the mind that is not criminal, and an overwhelming number of bad thoughts leads to crime. We must reduce bad thoughts. The criminal will always think bad thoughts, as all people do. But people who are well-adjusted and do not get sent to correctional institutions do not have a surplus of bad thoughts. We need to take the deviant and replace their deviant thoughts with good thoughts, responsible thoughts that lead to efficiency. The deviant is a person who does not value the five pillars of modern society.

The Five Pillars of Modern Society

1. Go to work and do your job.

2. Care for your children.

3. Pay your bills

4. Obey the law.

5. Buy products.

If a person does these five things every day of their life they will be responsible and achieve a high level of efficiency. These are the cornerstones of modern society. If everyone in a modern society does these five things, then modern society will run smoothly.

The Five Pillars of Modern Society are not to be discussed with the deviants. They are only to be known by the employees of the institution in charge of taking care of the deviants.

Urine Tests

Imad looked at me and said, "Now we are going to do a urine test. Urine tests are very important because we need to know if the residents have been doing drugs. If we find out that they are doing drugs, that is bad."

"Okay," I said.

"We test for many drugs. We test for MDMA, marijuana, meth, Xanax, painkillers. You name it, we test for it."

"Okay."

Imad continued, "We got a memo today. Today we are giving urine tests to Dave Morgan and Sherwood Burke. We have to call them up here and then they are not allowed to leave until they urinate. They have to sit at that table." He pointed at the table. It was a small round table with plastic, uncomfortable seats.

Imad said, "They sit at that table and when they have to pee they tell us. When they pee I will show you what to do then."

Imad called down to the lower floor. A few minutes later, Dave Morgan and Sherwood Burke came up.

Dave Morgan was a feeble-looking man. His head was

shaved. He was in his mid-twenties but still had pimples. He had badly-done tattoos on his arms and legs. He was wearing what looked like a gym outfit. He couldn't focus his eyes. His eyes darted around and never settled on a specified location. He said to Imad, "Why am I up here?"

Imad said, "Urine test."

"I'm not on drugs. I've been in here for four months. How am I supposed to do drugs while I'm locked up in here?"

"Sit down at that table," Imad said.

"I didn't bring up anything to read or do. Can I go down and get something?"

"No, sit down at the table and tell me when you have to urinate."

"I just went, it could take hours."

Imad handed him a Styrofoam cup and said, "Drink water."

Dave Morgan held the cup and said, "Drink water?"

"Yes, sit down and stop arguing, or I'll write you up."

"What?"

"Sit down," Imad said.

Sherwood Burke came up to Imad and said, "Yes." Sherwood Burke stood there looking at Imad, his eyes were focused on Imad's face. You could tell that he was thinking about ripping Imad's face off. If Burke wanted to he could. He was six foot two and had a thick Scottish frame. I felt afraid of him.

Sherwood Burke sat down without question. He knew the procedure.

Imad said to me after they sat down and were out of hearing distance, "Stand here and watch them but don't talk to them. If they have a question, tell them to ask me. If they try to engage you in conversation, don't speak. If you allow them to speak to you they will try to manipulate you. Think of these assholes as manipulation machines. They aren't like us. These assholes are the scum of the earth. If you don't believe me, then read their Resident Profiles on the computer. I'm gonna go smoke and sign some documents."

Imad left me with the two criminals. I wasn't supposed to speak to them, only watch, make sure they didn't go anywhere. Imad said this could take hours. That was my job for the day, to watch two men I had never met sit at a small round table, waiting for them to notify me that they needed to urinate, then I would tell Imad, and then they would each urinate into a cup.

I sat down at a computer and looked up their Resident Profiles.

Dave Morgan's Resident Profile

Crimes: Had stolen an X-Box from Sears, he has not paid child support for the last year, once received stolen property, got caught with a handgun, when the police were trying to pull him over for going five miles over the speed limit he tried to get away. When the police found him he had a pound of marijuana in the car.

Education: He made it to the 8th grade and dropped out. He is attempting to get his GED inside NEOTAP.

Beliefs: He believes he is a hard worker and a quick learner. He does not have any religious beliefs, does not know why he is alive, does not care why he is alive, doesn't show concern for his or anyone else's life. He does not have the capability to murder, but will steal anyone's money, even his own grandmother's, if he is given the chance.

Children: He has two children he rarely ever sees. He works under the table or sells drugs so he does not have to pay child support. He never sees his children and shows little concern for them. He will state that he wants to see his children and take care of them, but shows no evidence of ever actually caring about them.

Special Things: He complains a lot, talks a lot, never listens, and does not care. NEOTAP must make him see himself as a person living amongst other persons, and that he is not just a collection of psychological feelings that Morgan wants to satisfy.

Sherwood Burke's Resident Profile

Crimes: He has the habit of getting into bar fights. Even though he often wins these bar fights he has the intelligence to know when to stop before he kills the person he is fighting. He has stolen repeatedly from clothing stores. Last time he was caught stealing he had an ounce of marijuana on him. It can be assumed that he has stolen hundreds of times from clothing stores and never been caught. He states that he does not care about stealing from corporate clothing stores because corporations are harmful to society anyway.

Education: Sherwood Burke served four years in the Marines and has fought in Iraq. While in the military and for a short time after, he went to college, earning junior-level credits. He plans on returning to college eventually. He is above average intelligence but he is emotionally unstable, and does not concern himself with procedure.

Beliefs: Sherwood Burke believes that he does not matter. He states that his life has been nothing but trying to survive in a world that does not care about him. He has woken up every day of his life and been forced to figure out what other people want, forced to adapt their needs not his. He said that he started to commit crimes because it made him feel control over his life and to feel alive.

Children: None.

Special Things: He will behave normally and follow procedure for long periods of time but then when a certain mood takes over, he will act like a maniac. NEOTAP must make Burke recognize when the maniac feelings come over him, and get him to repress those feelings.

I read their Resident Profiles and then looked at them. They were both sitting there. I walked closer to them but did not talk, but stood close enough to hear them talk.

Dave Morgan said, "This is stupid, I didn't do no drugs. Why they gotta bother me. This is stupid. How am I gonna do drugs, I ain't got no drugs here. There ain't no drugs anywhere in here."

"It is procedure. They do this to everyone," Burke said.

"Procedure, what the fuck is a procedure?"

"I think it is an old French word for control."

"French, what the fuck is French? I don't wanna sit here. I don't have anything to do. I keep drinking water and I still don't have to pee."

Burke sat there, staring.

Morgan looked at me and said, "Why do we have to sit here? I ain't got no drugs in here. There ain't no drugs. I'm done with drugs. I'm improved. I don't do drugs. Why are you still drug testing me?"

I stood there in silence.

Morgan said, "Why don't you say something? I don't have to pee. Why can't I get a magazine from my room? You could follow me. I wouldn't pee the whole time. I would be a good boy. You could follow me and watch. My room is like twenty feet away. I promise I won't get any fake pee from here and there. You could follow me."

"He won't respond," Burke said.

"Why?" Morgan asked.

Burke said, "Because he is a new hire. New hires aren't allowed to talk to residents for two weeks."

Morgan looked at me and said, "You aren't allowed to talk."

I said nothing. I felt like a Buckingham Palace guard. I imagined myself standing before Buckingham Palace wearing a scarlet tunic and a giant bearskin hat. Instead of guarding the queen and the 1,300-year-old monarchy of Britain, I was guarding these two grown men from urinating. I would use every fiber in my being to stop these men from illegally urinating or going to their rooms to get something to read. I was on guard. I was a man with a task to keep my country strong. I was contributing to society.

Burke said, "He isn't even allowed to say no. No would imply you have power over him. He doesn't have to say anything to us."

"This is bullshit," said Morgan.

"I was in the military. This is how it works. Hierarchy is everything," Burke said.

"You weren't in the fucking military."

"I drove a tank in Baghdad. I conquered an ancient city. How many ancient cities have you conquered?"

"Fuck you, Burke."

Burke looked at me. "How about you? You conquer any ancient cities?" he said. I could tell that everything he did was calculated. He was warming me up. He knew I had never been in corrections. He knew that I had just arrived from a local college. He knew that I was from the middle-class because NEOTAP didn't hire poor people. He also knew that no self-respecting wealthy person would work in corrections. But he didn't know if I was a power-tripping monster or just some guy looking for work. He wanted to test me. He wanted to see if I would break and speak with them. "I asked you a question," he said.

I stood there in silence. My only concern was that they were not allowed to urinate.

Morgan said, "Why are you bothering him? He's probably going to log everything you say."

Burke was still staring at me. He said, "I have to urinate now."

"Okay, I'll get Imad."

Imad got a urine testing cup out of a cabinet. He put on a pair of latex gloves and instructed me to put on a pair too. He said, "These guys have a million diseases. You don't want to catch one." Imad showed the cup to Burke and said, "This is your cup. I am now taking it out of the package."

Burke watched him take it out of the package.

Imad wrote Burke's name on it, along with his social security number and the time and date.

Imad held up a red sticker. "This is the red sticker that seals the urine test cup. After the urine test is complete and the red sticker is placed on the cup, you must sign the red sticker. Do you understand?"

"Yes."

Imad called in a guard to watch Morgan since I needed to see how the urine test was conducted and couldn't stay back to watch Morgan.

When the guard arrived, Burke, Imad, and I walked to the bathroom.

In the bathroom, Imad said to Burke, "Wash your hands."

Burke washed his hands.

Then Imad directed Burke to go to the corner stall. Imad said, "All urine tests must be given in this stall. As you can see there is a mirror there so you can watch them pee." Imad handed the cup to Burke. Burke looked at the cup and said, "How much do you want me to fill?"

"Halfway," Imad said.

Burke turned to the toilet and unzipped his pants.

Imad said to me, "Stand here and look in the mirror and watch him. You must look at his penis. You must see if he has secret urine from another person or animal urine hidden in his pants. You must watch the urine leave his penis. You must watch it."

I stood over there and looked into the mirror. I said, "I can't see his penis."

Imad said, "Move in closer, get his penis in eyeshot. You must be looking at his penis."

I moved closer. There was his penis.

I stared at his penis. Burke said, "Can you see my penis? I don't want to do this until you can see my penis."

"Yes, I can see your penis."

Burke began to urinate.

The sound of the urine hitting the cup made me a little sick. The urine was a dark yellow.

I didn't want to watch him pee. It occurred to me that I went to college and learned about Rousseau and the structure of the Chinese government and constitutional law, got good grades and never once had to learn about urine tests. I was not educated to give urine tests. I started to think that my education was pointless. Instead of learning about the geography of Iran or the history of Russia, I should have been learning the science of urine tests. The science of watching urine leaving another man's penis. I owed $25,000 in student loans so that I could monitor urine tests.

After Burke finished peeing in the cup, he handed the cup to me and smiled. I didn't want to hold the cup of urine.

I took the urine over to the sink. Imad directed Burke to wash his hands. Burke never spoke to Imad. Burke knew the deal. He knew that the whole time he was there, he was being watched. The urine test wasn't the real test. Behaving normally during the urine test was what mattered. Burke knew he would pass the urine test. Imad knew it too. Imad asked Burke to sign the red sticker. Burke took a pen and signed it and smiled. He asked politely, "Can I go?"

"Yes," Imad said.

Imad was a master at talking to the residents. He never gave them information, never allowed them to speak or ask questions. Imad loved his job. He loved directing the residents. He considered himself a leader of men.

Imad and I went to a staff bathroom. He held up the urine test cup and ripped off the red sticker sealing the cup. Imad said, "He is clean."

"Do we tell them if it isn't?"

"I will show you the next steps. First we throw it away. We pour the urine out into the toilet and then throw the cup into the biohazard waste disposal bin. Then we sign four forms and log the result on the computer."

Imad brought me into the office and got out four different books and signed NEG on all of them and signed his name.

Then he went on the computer and logged that Burke completed a urine test and that the result was NEG and that Burke complied peacefully with all demands. Imad said to me, "See, everyone can see the log book on the computer. Everyone here checks on the log book. Somebody will read it and see today's result was negative. If it was positive, then something would happen, but it wouldn't be us responsible for it anymore."

"What would happen?"

"Something," said Imad.

"Who is in charge of that something?"

"Somebody."

"Has anyone ever failed a urine test in here?"

"Yes."

"How many people since you've worked here?"

"I have never seen somebody fail one, but I have heard about it."

I stood there.

Imad was a master at his job. He said, "I need to go back to my office and sign more forms."

Imad returned to his office.

Burke's Penis

I was sitting in the command center looking at the log book on the computer. Heidelberg approached me and said, "Mike, please come with me."

I got up and followed Heidelberg. I was terrified. Having a conversation out of nowhere with Heidelberg was very bad. No one at NEOTAP openly despised Heidelberg. Everyone at NEOTAP knew that everything was being filmed and that everyone was a spy. The residents were the worst spies of all and they were everywhere. A resident would tell on you faster than a fellow employee. The residents hated the guards even if we didn't have weapons or beat them. The residents considered everyone in authority an asshole.

Heidelberg brought me into the same small room where I read *Reality Conversion*. Heidelberg was not smiling. Her face was just mean. A mean-looking white face staring at me. I was getting paid $11.30 an hour. Part of my job was putting up with being watched by her. Then her mean face spoke. "We were watching on the video and we saw that you picked your nose."

I did not know how to respond.

"Did you pick your nose?"

"When?"

"It was on video, we have it recorded. Michael, you must understand, we can see everything you do. We saw you pick your nose. We must assume that you aren't taking your job seriously. No serious worker of NEOTAP would ever pick their nose."

"I'm sorry."

"We don't think you listen."

I sat there in silence, not knowing what I should say. I was listening to her.

"I also got word that you didn't look at Burke's penis when he took the urine test. Is that true?"

"I looked at his penis." I knew I couldn't argue with her. That was absolutely not allowed.

"Imad said you did not look at his penis. He said you were not listening which led to you not looking at Burke's penis."

"I looked at his penis."

"I don't believe you. Imad has been with NEOTAP for five years. He knows how this job works. He understands NEOTAP, he believes in NEOTAP. We don't believe that you believe in NEOTAP."

"I believe in NEOTAP."

Heidelberg pulled three photos out of a bag.

She put the photos on the desk and said, "Look at these photos."

Each photo depicted a penis.

Each penis was white and flaccid.

She said, "As you can see, these are penises."

I looked at her in puzzlement and then looked back at the three penises.

She said, "I want you to look at these penises for a long time. I want you to tell me which penis is Burke's."

Heidelberg looked extremely serious. She cared whether I got this right or not. I thought of the guards at the Buckingham Palace. I wondered if they were ever forced to look at penises. It occurred to me that, to work for the government, one had to look at penises sometimes.

I stared at the photos and tried to remember what Burke's penis looked like.

Heidelberg said, "Close your eyes, see Burke's penis in your head. See it, feel it, smell it."

I ran through a process of elimination. Penis B had a mole which I didn't remember being on Burke's penis. Penis A was really dark, like maybe Southern Italian. Penis C was pale with a little bit of girth. I said, "Penis C."

Heidelberg picked up the penis pictures without showing emotion and put them back in her bag.

"Is that right?" I said.

"Michael."

"Yes."

"You must learn that it is not important for you to ask questions. Nobody needs for you to ask questions. Your job is to follow procedure. Following procedure does not require questions."

"Okay."

"Imad says you don't ask enough questions."

"I don't?"

"Yes."

"I will try to ask more questions."

"Good."

Body Count

I walked into the main office at eight in the morning. I put my coat up and sat in a cushioned chair at a conference table.

I sat there drinking a pumpkin-spice latte, waiting for the staff briefing. A staff briefing happened every day at the shift changeover. The preceding and proceeding shifts would discuss any new developments. Some of the staff had already arrived, but they didn't speak to me. We waited for Imad to arrive.

Finally, Imad came and started the briefing. "Recently we've had a lot of incidents. It has been pretty crazy around here. Lisa Hefner got seven meatballs for lunch instead of six," he said.

A woman named Nisreen said, "Yup, that's her all right."

Imad continued. "Joe Rupert was three minutes late for his work assignment. We need to watch him."

A man named Lawrence said, "Yeah, we really need to get on these guys. These guys really need to know who is in charge. Those work assignments are vital to the operations of NEOTAP."

Imad continued. "Bob Packwood was joking around

and called Mark Vander 'shorty.'"

Except for Imad, everyone laughed because it was true. Mark Vander was only five feet tall.

Imad said, "But that must not be allowed. There are no nicknames in NEOTAP. We must teach them responsibility. Angie Lambert told Lakisha that she was cute yesterday. There is no lesbianism in NEOTAP. Residents need to be minding their own programs and focus on their own lives, not trying to have sex with other residents. Howard Evans got a letter from somebody who used to be in NEOTAP. Howard Evans's mail will be sent to his case manager now. We must watch the mail of residents. Okay, let's go get 'em."

Lawrence pumped a fist in the air and yelled, "Let's get 'em!"

The staff seemed really excited about guarding the residents, about watching their every behavior. It occurred to me that they really liked this type of work. It had not occurred to me to enjoy working at NEOTAP. They had a general feeling of unity amongst each other. This unity gave them power, this unity of us against them gave them a sense that they were part of something bigger than themselves. We weren't getting paid enough to enjoy the American Dream, but we were expected to defend it.

My job for the morning was to do a body count. A body count consisted of printing out a piece of paper with everyone's name on it. Then I had to go around finding everybody and marking their name "in."

I went to the lower level; the residents were sitting around, looking bored. Some were reading, some were having small conversations. I walked up to a table of four and wrote their names down. One guy, Rex Tugford, had tattoos of snakes all over his head. He said to me, "I can't wait to get out of here, I can't wait to see my kids."

I said, "Sounds good, Rex."

After finishing the body count, I noticed that Sherwood Burke was missing from the paper. I couldn't remember him leaving so I went up to Imad and said, "Where is Sherwood Burke? He wasn't recorded in the body count."

Imad looked at me blankly and said, "Your position does not require you knowing that."

I stood there, confused. "Is he here or not here?"

"Your position does not require you knowing that."

I logged the body count into the computer and then checked the NEOTAP log to see if there was a reason Sherwood Burke was missing. The log said nothing. Sherwood Burke was gone. He had disappeared.

I found Nisreen and asked her, "Where did Sherwood Burke go?"

"I'm not concerned," she replied.

Before I could ask any more questions, Imad came up and said, "Mike, clean Sherwood Burke's locker. Put everything in a garbage bag and stick it in the closet where we keep residents' possessions."

The chance of looking at Sherwood Burke's locker fascinated me.

I put on plastic gloves and got a garbage bag. I went to Sherwood Burke's room. The room contained six bunk beds. The rooms were not decorated. There was one window without a curtain. In the morning if the sun was shining, a bright light would come through the window and wake everybody up.

Above every bed was a corkboard where the residents could tack up pictures of their family and lovers. I walked over to Sherwood Burke's cork board. Nothing was on it. It was empty. I looked at the other residents' corkboards. They had pictures of their kids on the board, birthday cards, and sexy but clothed pictures of their girlfriends and wives.

I opened up Sherwood Burke's locker. I removed the hygiene products and clothes and put them in the garbage bag. At the bottom of the locker were notebooks and folders. I looked at the folders. They were full of papers concerning his anger management classes. I threw them in the garbage bag. He had no letters. Usually everyone had letters, but he had none. He had one picture of him standing with three guys on an army base. It said in black pen on the back, "Iraq 2004." He was smiling and looked happy. I threw that picture in the garbage bag. There was a copy of Maxim and Plato's *The Laws* and Machiavelli's *The Prince*. Both were old Penguin Classics versions from the eighties. And a copy of *Genghis Khan and the Making of the Modern World*. All three of the books had passages highlighted and notes written in the margins. Then I found a notebook with the word "Theory" on the cover. I opened it up and found page after page of handwritten theories on things. I decided to keep it. I wanted to know what it was like being in NEOTAP. Was it horrible or helpful? I brought the garbage bag to the closet and snuck the notebook into the office, folded it up and put it in my coat. I knew that cameras most likely saw me but I was hoping that no one was watching them when I did it.

Alone in my room, before I went to sleep, I opened Sherwood Burke's notebook.

A brief excerpt from the notebook of Sherwood Burke

NEOTAP does not ask us to make our situation better, they do not train us to fight for unions or vote for politicians that may better our lives. They do not help us understand why we are poor, why our parents were poor, why there are so many of us stuck in correctional facilities. Instead they teach us to go to work for eight dollars an hour with no health care. The mission of NEOTAP is not to help us but to get us to love the system that makes our lives terrible. The mission of NEOTAP is for us to do our duty, which is to be complacent, docile like subdued children. They aren't teaching us to make our lives better; they are teaching us to be a responsible class of Untouchables.

Outside Break

I called over the walkie-talkie to let the criminals out. I sat on a bench and watched the criminals. Watching criminals was boring. Imad told me that watching criminals was of the most vital importance, that they were constantly figuring out ways to cause trouble. That they had only one intention and that was to do something bad. The criminals sat down at picnic tables and on the benches and would talk peacefully. They couldn't smoke because the state ruled that smoking was illegal in prisons.

Bob Packwood and Rex Tugford sat near me and I could hear them talking about Sherwood Burke.

Bob Packwood said, "Dude, he's gone. He ain't here anymore."

Red responded, "Yeah, man, he just fucking disappeared."

"He was a good guy. He never caused any problems."

"No, he didn't bother me."

Bob Packwood was a tall, Irish-looking monster. He had the same buzzcut they all did, and his body was solid muscle from years of exercising in and out of jail. In his profile it stated that he had never really done drugs his whole life until he was in a car wreck and was laid up for a year. During that year he became dependent on oxies to calm the pain. After he healed he still loved oxies and became a full-time addict, lost his job, his kids, and ended up in jail for possession of drugs. Rex was covered in tattoos and had committed an enormous amount of crime. He was thirty-six and since the age of sixteen he had spent twelve of the last twenty years in correctional facilities. He stole from stores, robbed several gas stations, stabbed a man in the arm once, dealt drugs, ran drugs, sold firearms illegally, ran from the police, punched a cop, and owed $22,000 in child support. But his face didn't show signs of anger or bitterness. I felt bitter about having to pay student loans but he felt okay about spending the majority of his adult life in prison.

Bob and Rex noticed I was listening and Rex said, "You know where Sherwood is?"

"No, do you?"

Rex responded, "Man I thought you would know. People be disappearing from here all the time. It's bullshit."

Bob said, "Yeah, what is this shit? You wake up and somebody is gone. Like how does somebody just disappear?"

"They don't tell me those things," I said.

"No shit they don't, cuz you ain't nothing big yet," Rex said.

"I wish I knew what Sherwood did, because I wouldn't do that thing he did, you know. I want to finish my program. I want to get out and be a normal person," said Bob.

Rex said, "Yeah, normal, I wanna be normal. You hear that, Mike? Put that in your log book. Make sure they know I want to be normal."

I looked at them and said nothing. There was no way I could respond. I shouldn't have said anything. I was trapped.

After the outside break was over I went into the office

and everyone was eating pizza. There were four boxes of pizzas and each pizza had different toppings. Heidelberg and Imad were standing there, just smiling. Heidelberg had put a small TV in the room so we could watch football all day. Her smile was so big and nice. I didn't understand it. Then Heidelberg said, "Hey Mike, get a piece of pizza. Everyone loves pizza."

I felt confused and went over and picked up a slice of a pizza.

Heidelberg said, "How is your grandpa?"

"He's good."

Heidelberg laughed and said, "When I was young I spent a lot of time with my dad's parents. They lived next door so when my parents weren't home or when there was nothing going on at my house I would go over there. My grandma and I would make cookies and brownies together and my grandpa would tell me about being in World War 2."

"That sounds kind of like my grandma. All she wanted to do was feed me, like she constantly asked me, 'Mike are you hungry, do you need anything to eat Mike, I don't think you ate enough Mike, do you want me to make you some food?'"

We both laughed about grandmas.

Then I said, "How is your kid, Rachel?"

"Oh, he is doing great. I am teaching him the alphabet and he is learning it really well. He is so smart."

Then Imad came over and stood there eating a piece of pizza.

Rachel said, "How is your new wife?"

Imad said, "Everything seems to be going smoothly."

Rachel said, "When are you going to have a kid?"

"The next time you give me a raise," said Imad.

We all laughed.

Then Heidelberg said, "Well, I have to go to a meeting and I've already eaten my max of three pieces, even though I know I could eat five. Gotta watch my weight in my old age."

I said, "You aren't old. What are you, like thirty-one?"

"I'm thirty-six, Mike, but thanks for those five years."

Heidelberg left. It was just Imad and I standing there, and Imad said, "Before I have a kid, I have to get my wife to stop spending all our money on clothes. Man, all she does every Saturday is go to the mall and buy clothes. I don't even know what she does with all those clothes. Most of the time when I see her she is wearing jogging pants and a sweater. But she has massive amounts of clothes, I think she might be a hoarding addict. Have you seen that show *Hoarding*?"

"Yeah."

"Yeah man, my wife, she hoards clothes. I wish she would like hoard pizza and beer, but instead she hoards clothes. I don't know what I'm gonna do."

"Yeah, women, they are crazy with that shopping. My ex-girlfriend shopped constantly, spent tons of money, and then when we went I had to pay for both of our meals because she spent all her money on clothes."

"I know, I know."

Then Imad walked away.

I felt confused by the whole pizza event. Everyone acted really nice and human in their own way. I walked back to my post and watched the residents. The residents received no pizza. They sat staring at the walls or reading magazines.

Jay Riddick

Around two in the afternoon I was standing in the office looking at the schedules for the next week, and I noticed that Jay Riddick was gone. His name had disappeared from the schedule. I remembered in the morning that his name had been there. It said Jay Riddick and all the days and times he was scheduled to work the next week. I didn't understand. Jay Riddick had disappeared. An employee could disappear just like the residents.

I looked around the office and didn't see anyone but Monica Whitten, the IT person. Monica Whitten graduated from college with a computer science degree and had been working for NEOTAP for two years. She was young and pretty. I kind of had a crush on her. I thought she was nice.

I said, "Monica, where did Jay Riddick go?"

"Maybe he went on vacation."

"No, he just went on vacation."

"I don't know."

"The other day Sherwood Burke disappeared."

"Who's that?"

"A resident."

"Oh."

"Now Jay has disappeared. That guy was nice, and now he is just gone."

"Go ask Imad, maybe he'll tell you."

"Yeah."

I left the office. I found Imad standing by himself. He was just standing there with his hands on his hips, gazing out like he was the master of the world and not a small Arab man who could get his ass kicked by every one of the residents. I said to Imad, "Imad, where did Jay go? Is he still on vacation?"

Imad didn't look at me. "Jay doesn't work here anymore."

"How come?"

"He doesn't work here anymore."

He never looked at me. I walked back to the office and told Monica, "Imad said he doesn't work here anymore."

"Why doesn't he work anymore?"

"I don't know. Imad wouldn't say," I said.

Monica said, "You know, I have access to all of the documents from my laptop at home. Do you want to look at them tonight?"

"Yeah, that sounds great."

We made plans to meet up after work.

Half an hour before my shift was over, Imad came over to me and said, "Go to Heidelberg's office." I knew it was bad. Heidelberg did not believe in positive reinforcement. I realized that I had worked there for three weeks and not once did someone tell me I was doing a good job. They notified me immediately when I was doing a bad job, but not when I was doing a good job. I didn't know what a good job was, I only knew what a bad job was. I had never worked for an institution that never gave positive feedback. I had worked for mega-corporations and local places, and both had notified me if I was doing things properly. But NEO-TAP did not concern itself with helping the employee know when they were doing a good job. That wasn't procedure.

I sat before Heidelberg. I sat there knowing I had a bachelor's degree, that I graduated with a 3.4. My professors liked me, people with doctorates liked me. I could easily get a recommendation from a good amount of professors. I was told by my professors that I would have a bright future. I had won employee of the month at several of my jobs. No one had ever complained about my performance at work or in college. Getting yelled at constantly confused me. I knew I wasn't allowed to speak first so I waited for Heidelberg.

Heidelberg, looking very angry, said, "I heard about what happened in the bathroom today."

"Yes." I knew I had to say yes. Yes was the appropriate reply.

"Imad called meds, correct?"

"Yes."

"He told you over the walkie-talkie to get Sanders, correct?"

"Yes."

"You called back over the walkie-talkie that resident Sanders was shaving."

I remembered what happened. Imad called one o'clock meds at 12:30, not one o'clock. I went to the bathroom and Sanders was shaving. I told Sanders that Imad wanted him for meds. Sanders replied that Imad was not following procedure, and that he had the right to shave because he was following the rules. I called back on the walkie-talkie that Sanders was shaving. Imad yelled over the walkie-talkie, "Tell Sanders to come now or he will be written up."

Heidelberg said, "I know that Imad did not follow procedure and start meds on time, but what you must understand, Mike, is that hierarchy trumps procedure. If someone who is your superior tells you to do something, even if it contradicts procedure, then you must do it, and the resident must do it. If Edward Choffin comes in here right now and tells me to do jumping jacks and sing 'Paradise City' by Guns N' Roses, then I have to do that. You know why, Mike?"

"Because hierarchy trumps procedure."

"That is correct. Also, there is one more item we need to talk about."

"Okay," I said.

"You asked Imad where Jay Riddick went today."

"Yes."

"You have a serious problem with listening. You don't listen. You don't need to know those things. Those things are not your business. Everyone in this establishment has 'their business.' I have my business, and you have your business. Everything you do is my business, everything you know is my business, everything you think and feel is my business. Everything that is my business is none of your business. Nothing that pertains to me pertains to you. Everything that pertains to you also pertains to me. Do you understand?"

"Yes."

"We have had word from other staff members that you don't take things seriously. That you don't believe that this is a serious job. This is a very serious job."

I wanted to say that counting sad drug addicts wasn't that serious. That no one cared about these people. The only time people cared about the residents was when one of them committed a crime. Politicians didn't care about their lives, corporations didn't care about their lives, and the media didn't care about their lives. Heidelberg didn't even care about them. She had a job that paid well, offered good health care, and gave her a chance to power-trip. She had her American Dream.

Heidelberg went on. "Every procedure is vital to this institution. If you don't do the body count right, people could escape. Do you know that? People could escape."

"Yes." Where could they go, seriously? I wanted to say 'seriously' too. It seemed like 'seriously' was a catch word when someone didn't have a point but wanted to make a point, and they knew they didn't have a point. They felt the pointlessness of their point and then said 'seriously' to make it a point.

"Do you understand how vital all this is? We are shaping the thoughts and behaviors of men and women who badly need to be reformed to live in society."

"Yes."

"Good. Now go back to work."

Monica Whitten Comes Over

I heard a knock on the door. I knew it was Monica. I went to the door and opened it. I felt like a sixteen-year-old, I was so excited to see her. She was dressed in street clothes and looked better than usual. I really liked Monica's smile and laugh. She seemed so kind, so polite. She seemed like the kind of person who would always do their duty to their friends and family, the kind of person who would give things up for other people. She would give time, she would give money, she would give it all to others and not think once about it.

Monica and I went into the kitchen where my grandfather was sitting. I introduced Monica by saying, "Grandpa, this is Monica."

The old man looked at her, smiled and said, "Monica, an ancient name, the name of Saint Augustine's mother, a woman of devout faith. It could be said that her faith was the faith that gave Saint Augustine the ideas and power to write those books that changed human history for a thousand years. She was the great muse of Saint Augustine, but also it might be related to the Greek word 'monos' meaning 'alone.'"

Monica stared at my grandfather and said, "Alone?"

"Yes, alone."

"Do you think one day I will be alone?"

"Sounds good."

We walked up to my bedroom and put her laptop on my bed. We lay on my bed on our bellies. I glanced at her body. She was small and skinny. She had a little peach butt that bulged in her leggings. I thought about her naked. I thought to myself, I want to lick her all over. I did not say that thought out loud.

She said, "Okay, I don't know if I should be doing this, but this sounds really fun. I hate NEOTAP anyway. The only thing that saves me is that I work for the IT department."

She opened the NEOTAP program and said, "What do you want me to look for?"

"Look for Sherwood Burke."

She brought up all the residents, all the past and present residents. She showed me that she could access all the logs on residents, all the documents written by their case workers, even all their juvenile records. She had complete access. I said, "Where is Burke though?"

Monica said, "I can't find him."

"He has to be in there."

"No, nothing. I've looked everywhere."

"Well, look up Jay Riddick."

Monica went to the employee records. She said, "Do you want to see your record?"

"Okay."

She brought up my record. There were reports on how I couldn't handle bathroom situations and a thing about me asking too many questions but at the same time not asking enough questions.

I said, "But where is Jay Riddick?"

"I don't know. I can see the names of several ex-employees, so he must be here somewhere."

"Okay, Google Sherwood Burke. He committed felonies. He must have things in the newspaper archives."

She Googled Sherwood Burke and nothing came up.

They had disappeared.

"This is really weird," I said.

"Yeah, it is."

We sat there for a while, confused. We were both people who went to college to become well-adjusted adults who paid their bills and taxes, but that didn't seem right. How did we find ourselves in a job where people disappear?

I asked Monica if she wanted to watch a movie on Netflix and she said, "Sounds good."

We sat in my room watching a movie.

Monica said, "What if we disappear one day?"

"What?"

"What if we disappear?"

"Do you think the IT person would disappear?"

"I don't know. Jay disappeared."

"Yeah, you're right."

"Should we quit our jobs?" she said.

"I put out more applications but nobody is hiring."

"Yeah, you're right."

After we watched a movie on Netflix, we fell asleep. We fell asleep with our clothes but before that she cuddled me. One of her small dark arms went over my chest and held me. I grasped her forearm with affection and we fell asleep.

The Criminal Thoughts of
Sherwood Burke

I lay in bed one night and read more of Sherwood Burke's notebook.

Sherwood Burke wrote:

These are my real criminal thoughts. NEOTAP is trying to remove my thoughts and fill me with new thoughts. I still retain my thoughts. Corrections have taken all my money, my ability to work, my ambition, my ability to even resemble a human being. They control all my behaviors, they analyze all my behaviors, but they will not get to my thoughts. I still have my thoughts.

Criminal Thought #1. I want to get a woman pregnant. I will find the fattest stupidest woman I can find. I don't care what race she is, probably white. If you have been to prison, fat white girls are easy. All you gotta do is show them some prison tats and a fat white trash girl will fuck you. I will get the nastiest woman I can find. A woman I know for sure will not be responsible for the child. She won't even talk to the child, she won't even take the child to the park, she won't even get a job at McDonald's to at least have some money to buy the child a Christmas present. No, she will scam the government out of every dollar she can. Yeah, that kind of woman, I want that one. She is going to be so nasty. I will get her pregnant. I will beat her when she is pregnant. She will take it because she is used to getting beat. I will ask her how much her last boyfriend beat her and then beat her less than him, so she feels like she has a better situation. Then when the child is born I will leave her. I think I will go back to prison. I will steal something from a Wal-Mart like a video game system or a bookshelf. The fat girl who gave birth to my child will write me letters in prison, she will tell me she loves me, I will tell her to send me money, she will do it because she is a fucking asshole. I will laugh the whole time. During the whole time I am in prison she will be fucking other men. She won't tell me she is fucking other men. I will use this as ammunition so when I get out I can leave her and not feel guilty. She will say, "I sent you money the whole time you were in." I will respond, "I don't care, you were fucking every Tom, Dick and Harry in the trailer park." It will be really funny. I will leave her, then I will get a job working under the table as a landscaper in the summer and in the winter I will work at a car wash under the table. I won't pay child support. I will do lots of drugs and never see my kid. It will be really funny.

Criminal Thought #2. I will become a pastor at an evangelical church when I get out. I will tell them I had been in prison for many years and during those many years I spent many hours studying the Bible, which is true. I was stuck in a jail for six months once awaiting trial and the jail library had a bunch of mystery and romance novels and nothing remotely good, so I was stuck reading the

Bible for six months. I read the whole damn thing from Genesis to Revelation four times. I wrote a whole notebook on the Bible, it got lost when I transferred from the jail to the prison, I didn't care. I would prove to the evangelicals that I knew my Bible. I wouldn't ask questions about the animals on the boat or if poverty was actually a necessity. I would simply quote from it and show proficiency. I would tell them that I was saved by Jesus Christ. They wouldn't ask for evidence. They don't care about evidence. I would get a job as a pastor, maybe a youth pastor with all the young girls, oh yeah, good. They would give me a paycheck biweekly and I would make connections in the church to get a job. I would behave normally the whole time, and that would be my crime. I'd tell everyone that I was saved, I had the Holy Ghost. I would teach the kids about the Holy Ghost, become obsessed with the Holy Ghost. Work my way up in the church, from youth pastor to traveling pastor, to head pastor. I would be making tons of money being a head pastor at one of those mega-churches. I would get a Christian wife, we would move into a nice house and drive nice cars. I would give long sermons on abortion and how homosexuals were the scourge of society. I would make up elaborate sermons on how homosexuality caused the national debt crisis, it would make perfect sense, everyone would believe me. I would feel great about all the lying. My whole life would be a terrible lie and lots of people would love it. After I convinced everyone to love me I would do something horrible, I would start smoking weed and intentionally get caught doing it by the police. It would ruin everything, everybody would be sad and talk about how I backslid, oh god it would be great. I would go back to prison and I would love it.

Criminal Thought #3. I stood staring at the window of my cell for three minutes today until that stupid new hire Mike told me that I had to go downstairs. Mike is such a fuckhead. He probably went to college and graduated and feels a sense of pride that he functions. He looks at us and knows we are scum. He knows he has never got arrested, the loser has never even got a DUI, what a fuck. Mike doesn't look happy though: he does look kind of depressed, his shoulders are hunched over. He doesn't know how to show authority. He might be different. I said to Mike, "You look depressed." He stood there, he didn't say anything. He looked like he wanted to cry. I stood there, waiting for an answer, I have time to wait, he doesn't have time to wait, he has to hurry up and make sure every room is clear of prisoners. But me, I have time, I have so much time that time isn't even an issue, I never look at calendars, I have no idea what fucking day it is. I live in a primitive time before the advent of calendars. The other prisoners ask me how long I have, I respond I don't know, because I don't. I don't care, Mike cares. Mike cares about time, he is probably counting the days until they give him health insurance, he is concerned with student loan bills that will come in the mail, he is concerned with his car payment, he is concerned all the time. I have no concerns. I am free, ha ha ha I am not. I would take out a gun and fire on Wall Street, the police would respond by firing back, they would shoot me, I would be Crispus Attucks, the first dead in the new revolution. I want to be Crispus Attucks. God, please let me be Crispus Attucks. I want to be discussed in 8th grade history classes for eternity.

I would like to serve the movement by getting killed. This would be my crime, a dirty scourge of humanity named

Sherwood Burke would get killed first. I would like to bleed to death in front of everyone, I want to go cold in front of the cameras. I want to be known as a person that got shot for political reasons. I want to be like Socrates, Jesus, Marcus Cicero and William Wallace, I want to be executed. But no one will let me die for a reason. Instead one day on some stupid Wednesday I will die in a gun fight over a drug deal gone wrong. Maybe I will outlive all this incarceration and die a peaceful old man with a wife, surrounded by children who love me. No that won't happen. I am determined and I take it very seriously that my life ends up shitty and stupid. Instead of marching on Washington or on Wall Street, I will play video games and smoke weed in living rooms full of thrift store furniture across America.

No one at Wall Street is thinking about me in this treatment prison. They don't care about me sitting in here rotting away, they probably think I am the scum of the earth too. I feel like scum, I feel like shit that needs to be wiped and flushed down the toilet. People look at me and think I am what is bad about America. I shouldn't join any protest, I should just stay in correctional facilities.

I have no voice.

Criminal Thought #4. After I get out of prison I will finish college and get an economics degree. I will go to New York and become a stock broker or a hedge funder, I will work my way up and achieve a high-level position. They will be very impressed with my organizational and troubleshooting skills. I will be in charge of things. I will have power. I will have so much money I will buy into large businesses and sit on the Board of Directors. I will give myself bonuses. I will rake in the cash. I will hire lawyers to find loopholes so I don't have to pay any taxes, it will be funny as shit. I will use the whole world as my playground, nothing will matter to me. I will hire lobbyists to deregulate my sector of the economy. I will not give a fuck about workers or nature. Fuck nature will be my slogan. Fuck the middle-class will be my slogan. Fuck everyone that gets in my way. I will only think about myself. I will pay my entry level employees $8.50 an hour, I don't care if they have mouths to feed or student loan payments, it doesn't matter to me. I will only put my factories in China and Mexico, and if I do put a factory in America it will be in places that give me a 15 year tax rebate. I hate taxes, I hate the worker. I will vote to have health insurance taken away from millions, I will vote so hospitals let people die who don't have health insurance. I will watch the masses burn. I will vote to take away social security; I will watch the elderly burn. I don't care if the elderly are homeless, fuck 'em, why don't they work harder? Take a fucking bath and get a job. That will be my slogan, my life-affirming prayer to the gods, take a fucking bath and get a job. They will take a bath and get a job making $8.50 an hour. I will make millions, maybe even billions. I will care about nothing, my life will be good and theirs won't, who gives a fuck. I will start giving giant campaign contributions to politicians, I will make them into what I want them to be, they will do what they are told. I will give them prestige and power, my prestige will be less than theirs but my power will be greater, who gives a fuck about virtue, about goodness, about harmony, when I will have all the power. I want all the power, I want everything, I will become part owner of oil companies and banks, then I will be like a god. I want to be like a god, I will rise so high that *Forbes* will put me on their cover. Everyone will know then I am truly a god to be feared. I will never allow a union at any of my businesses, I will never allow my workers to strike or ask for better pay. I will fire them all if they want anything. I will not pay my taxes, I will get offshore accounts to hide my money. It will be beautiful, but sadly it won't be criminal. Which means I can't do it, I only like to do criminal things.

Criminal Thought #5. I am sitting on the lower floor. I keep looking at my fellow prisoners. I realize I don't like them. I am like them, but I can't relate. They apologize for their crimes, they feel bad about doing horrible things. I don't feel bad. I tell my case manager that I feel bad to get out of here, but I don't actually feel bad at all. I don't give a fuck about all the people I ever beat up, I don't care about doing drugs, I like drugs, I don't care about the things I've stolen, I don't care. It doesn't bother me. Sometimes I sit and wait for it to bother me, I try to get the guilt to come, maybe swell some tears, but it doesn't come, nothing comes, I feel innocent. I need to rephrase that, I take full responsibility for my crimes, I did them, I chose to do them, but I don't consider your verdict valid. I went to prison because you have the weapons, the people with the weapons wanted me to go, so I went, that's all. I am here because of weapons. I don't have an army to combat you, therefore I must recognize your authority and do what you want.

I think I commit crimes because I don't know anything. I just don't know anything. I think knowing something implies 'a calling.' People in America have 'a calling.' God told Heidelberg that she should be in corrections, Heidelberg believed God and worked in corrections, she likes corrections, she likes power, she likes the snobbery of looking down on criminals. Now, of course God didn't call her to work in corrections, there was something about her childhood that led her to having a certain personality that found working in corrections very exciting. I have never found anything that exciting, nothing calls me. My personality finds the world and its work revolting. The modern world revolts me. Actually I don't know if the modern world revolts me. I don't know what revolts me. I wanted to be something, I know that, I grew up thinking that I would grow up and be something. I got good grades in school, I was impressive, I played football and scored touchdowns. I have had sex with attractive women. I have touched young firm breasts and ran my penis along long smooth legs. I have no worldview, I don't want to just believe in being Democrat or Republican, or Green, or atheist, or Christian, I don't want any of it. It all seems like shit made up by advertisers. But this is stupid, simpleminded complaining. I have never felt like I was part of the group. It doesn't matter what the group is, I just don't know how to feel like part of it. I want so badly at times to feel One with other people, I want to walk into a bar and start dancing with well-known friends, I want to go to a political rally and feel the force of collective participation, I want to go to a football game and cheer in unison for Our team to win, I want to go to a family gathering and be excited about seeing cousins and my aunt's new baby boy. I don't even feel good around criminals, criminals are my people, but I still feel odd around them. I feel like I am missing something in my heart, I don't think I am a sociopath, I am never really mean to people. I have empathy, I know that the resident supervisors have their own sad lives they must deal with, I know Heidelberg has her stupid problems, raising kids and being paranoid all the time has to be tough. I know this, I can calculate it all in my head. But I don't feel One with anyone. To have 'a calling' a person has to feel One with some group of people, for example: people

in corrections, people in marketing, people who are factory workers, people who are circus freaks, people who are
accountants, people who are housewives, people who are
in politics, people who are musicians, these are groups of
people. They all consider themselves a certain type of person that enjoys being around those other certain types of
people. I can't find my group, sometimes I think, I almost
have the group, I am almost there, sitting with my group,
feeling One, but then, it is gone. To be in a group means to
be part of Something, which means a person must believe
in that Something, they must have faith in that Something.
I have no faith which means I have no belief. How can I live
without belief, without faith? I don't know. My heart beats.
I keep living. I keep feeding myself, every day NEOTAP
feeds me and I eat. I am hungry, therefore I eat. If I really
wanted to die, I would find a way to kill myself, I could find
a way. But I don't kill myself. Every day passes and I still
have not killed myself. Why don't I kill myself I keep asking
myself. I have no answer, I keep eating and living, hoping
that someday I want to be in a group. That one day a group
comes and I feel One with it. And it feels natural. Oh man,
what a phrase, it feels natural. I want things to feel natural,
but they never do. Am I a fucking defective human being?
I read once that Ulysses S. Grant failed at every job he ever
did before he was general of the Union Army. Did he think
these thoughts? I worked in a factory once and there was
always a certain number of defective parts, am I a defective
part? Would I, before the age of modern medicine, have
died in childhood? I assume nature would have snuffed me
out. But modern medicine has kept me alive. I shouldn't be
here. I should be dead. I don't know if that makes sense. I
can't even believe my own logic anymore. Oh god, all this

logic. I want something poetic to happen to me. I don't want cognitive behavioral therapy to save me. I want some beautiful poetic experience to happen to me, where I know why I am here.

I remember working at a restaurant as a dishwasher, there were two dishwashers in their 40s who had been dishwashers since they were in their teens. But the dishwashers would go into deep conversations about which dishwashers were best, how to best wash dishes, how to best mop the floor at night. They were fucking serious about dishwashing. They believed in dishwashing.

This is the truth, this is my truth, this is what I believe, this is what I act on, my frame of reference, this is where my logic is derived. I can't do it. I just feel things, I know I feel things, I know that I don't make judgments but feel something and then act on it. I can't use logic concerning my feelings, my feelings demand musical notes, violins, guitar solos, the stomping of feet, poetic language, metaphors, poetic lines about birds or deserts or tree-crowded forests.

I read Sherwood Burke's thoughts. I wasn't like him. I wasn't so alienated and gloomy about life. I didn't mind taking orders as long as they were orders that I felt had reason behind them. I didn't mind working at restaurants, I didn't mind my professors asking for a stupid amount of citations for a five page paper. I didn't mind my parents. I went to holiday events and felt in general bored, but I still wanted to hear how my cousin Pete liked being in the Navy. I didn't mind helping my dad do yard work. It all seemed fine. The whole world was covered in games, evolution was a game, ecosystems were basically a game that the plants and animals had to figure out how to play. Why would my life be any different?

I looked through the notebook some more. I found pages and hand-drawn maps on the Civil War of Julius Caesar, on the empire of Attila the Hun, Genghis Khan, the early Ottoman Empire and the March of General Sherman. The maps were perfectly drawn out from memory. Notes were written on all of their empires and their strategic methods. Then there were over twenty maps of America. On one map a numbered dot signified every military installation in the inner forty-eight, what type of installation, if it was Marine, Air Force, Army or Navy, how many troops were there and what capabilities it had. Then there were maps of battle plans with lines drawn all over the inner forty-eight. It looked crazy. I started to think Sherwood Burke had lost his mind.

Cafeteria

Every day the residents had lunch. Because the residents were criminals, a guard had to watch them eat and make sure that they took the correct amount of food.

The cafeteria was small with thirty round tables and five chairs at each table.

On that day the residents were having hamburgers and green beans.

There were two pictures above the meal line demonstrating how the food should be placed on the plate. The hamburger patty had to on the plate next to the two buns. The ketchup had to go on another part of the plate. The burger was not allowed to be made for the sake of efficiency. I had to stand by the buffet and yell at the residents if they made their burger and didn't follow directions.

Everything went fine until Joe Newsome tried making his hamburger while still in line. "Joe," I said, "you can't make your burger. You have to bring the items to a table and assemble the burger there."

"What? Why can't I make a burger while in line? This is stupid."

"Joe, you are written up. This will be logged."

Joe just looked pissed.

At one point Heidelberg entered the cafeteria. She stood by the water machine and watched.

My whole body tensed up. I knew I was being watched. Everyone in the cafeteria starting having a mental breakdown. It was terrible. Workers and residents alike, we all knew that she was watching every one of us, waiting for the perfect moment to pounce on us, to reprimand us. She wanted us to do something wrong, she needed us to do something wrong, she wouldn't leave until somebody did something wrong. But who would it be? Who was going to be the one to piss off Heidelberg?

Somebody dropped a burger patty on the floor. It looked bad being there so I asked one of the residents to get a broom and clean it up. The resident came over and swept it up.

Heidelberg left immediately after. I watched her leave and sighed with relief. It didn't seem like anything bad happened in the short time she was there.

After lunch, Heidelberg found me and said, "My office, please."

I felt horrible. I wanted to cry. What did she want from me? I couldn't figure it out.

I sat in her office and tried to emotionally prepare for what was to come.

"Do you remember when the burger patty fell on the floor?"

"Yes," I said.

"Don't tell kitchen workers to sweep up burger patties so close to the buffet station. It could cause dust to come up from the floor and land on the food."

What was she talking about? I had worked at several

restaurants in college and never heard that once. That was completely absurd.

"I don't trust you, Mike. I don't think you believe in NEOTAP."

"I believe," I said, almost having a panic attack.

"You need to prove to me that you believe. You almost killed several residents today using a broom so close to the food."

I didn't know what to say. I had no idea what to say to Heidelberg. What she was saying was so strange, so impossible to respond to, but I just nodded and said, "Yes, I will never do that again."

"Good."

Then she dismissed me. I left feeling extremely confused.

Charlie Palmer

I did another body count in the morning. Two more people had disappeared. I didn't ask anyone where they went. I knew I would not get an answer. I didn't know what I was doing at NEOTAP. The place seemed terrible to me. Heidelberg wouldn't stop yelling at me, I was constantly being watched, people were disappearing, nobody ever talked about anything but fantasy football. I was in a constant state of tension. All my muscles were taut. I felt like crying all the time. But I wanted health care. I went to college and wanted to make at least eleven dollars an hour. If I quit, I was going to have to go back to restaurant work. Nobody was hiring political science majors. I thought when I was in college that I could at least get a job in an office, but I was told I needed six months of experience to do office work.

Monica and I couldn't even talk openly at work because it was against the policy of NEOTAP that NEOTAP employees speak to residents or each other outside of NEOTAP. Unless your conversation with another employee was about fantasy football, you were likely to get called into

Heidelberg's office. I woke up five days a week at six in the morning completely dreading going to NEOTAP. I would wake up and just hate my life. I would take a shower, put my clothes on, and drive the forty minutes to work. I would get to work and live in a constant state of fear that I was doing something wrong, then go home and do nothing at all. Sometimes I would lie on the couch for two hours alternately staring and taking naps to get NEOTAP out of my system. Then I would eat and eventually go to sleep. I didn't even bother calling my friends. All I could think about was NEOTAP and how I needed to behave properly at work for $11.30 an hour.

One day Imad came over to me and said, "Let's do mail."

I went over to the stack of envelopes and put them in little boxes. Every resident had their own box. After I completed putting the mail in the boxes, residents would come over and ask me for their mail, and I would hand it to them. But Imad was there.

Charlie Palmer came over and said, "May I have my mail."

I got up to get it and Imad said, "No."

I stood there looking at Imad.

Imad said, "Go sit down, Charlie."

I stood there for a second and then sat down.

Imad had a shit-eating grin on his face.

Charlie Palmer stood wearing a battered San Diego Chargers hoodie and a ripped pair of blue jeans, looking dejected.

There was no reason to not give Charlie Palmer his mail.

I was sitting next to a computer and looked up Charlie Palmer's profile:

Age: 47

Crimes: Charlie Palmer has four DUIs. He has been to court-mandated rehabilitation programs for drinking and refuses to stop drinking.

Education: Graduated high school.

Beliefs: Charlie Palmer doesn't believe in working. He has lived at his mother's house all his life. He has never married or had children. He has not held a job since 1998. Since then he has been living strictly off his mother. He is emotionally immature and confused by grownup activities. He confesses to drinking beer every day of his life.

Special Things: If he is yelled at, he will start crying.

I looked at Charlie Palmer. He was a sad piece of shit. When my father was forty-seven he had a wife, two kids, a house and a career. Charlie Palmer had nothing. Charlie Palmer had spent his life living off of his mother, but of course his mother may have trained him to be like that. His mother might have been the queen of enablers. She might have enabled all of his lazy behavior because she didn't want to be alone. But the question that kept occurring to me was this: did Charlie Palmer really deserve not to get his mail, to be power-tripped by Imad because of DUIs? Did he deserve to be put in a treatment facility for six months where everything he did was watched and monitored? He was an alcoholic, not a violent criminal. I looked at Imad. Several more people came up and asked for their mail and he said no. He didn't care. He thought it was all funny.

Charlie Palmer was a sad sack of a human being. There were a lot of rich people who lived off their parents' money and everyone thought they were awesome. There was a show on called *Keeping up with the Kardashians,* which was about rich kids who spend money all day. They made some of their own money, but they would have never made it without their rich parents helping them with their money and social connections. No one considered them bad people. I couldn't figure out the truth. The contradictions were making my brain grow tense and overworked. I wanted to leave, go home and sleep. But then I thought about getting health insurance and I just sat there.

Some people came over and asked for their mail and Imad gave it to them. Charlie Palmer tried again. He said, "I want my mail please."

"What did you say?" Imad said.

"I would like my mail please."

Imad handed him an envelope. Charlie Palmer opened it up in front of Imad. Inside there were two pictures of his sister's kids. Imad looked at the pictures and said, "Are these pictures on your property sheet?"

A property sheet was a piece of paper that listed all the property a resident could get for the week. If they didn't write the item on it, then they couldn't have that item.

Charlie Palmer said, "No, I didn't know I was getting any pictures so I didn't write them on my property sheet."

Imad took the pictures. "These are going in the storage closet. When you write down on the property sheet that you have two pictures, then I will give them to you."

"That won't be for a week."

"Are you arguing?"

"They're just pictures, Imad," Charlie Palmer said.

"No, they are property. You can't just get any piece of property you want whenever you want it. There are rules at NEOTAP."

"This is stupid."

Imad stood there, looking furious. "Stay there, Charlie."

Imad walked over to the phone and called Heidelberg.

Then Heidelberg came upstairs and said to Charlie Palmer, "To my office. Now."

They went to her office. I knew it was bad. Imad stood there with a shit-eating grin.

Charlie Palmer came out of Heidelberg's office crying.

The other guys looked at him but they didn't say anything. They knew if they said anything Imad would send them to Heidelberg's office, and they would also be crying.

Protest 2.0 Meeting

Monica and I decided to attend a meeting about Protest 2.0 at a local coffee shop. The Protest 2.0 protest had been going on for a month and my city had decided to start protesting the local banks. I had visited the coffee shop many times and just thought it would be interesting to hear a few speeches.

When Monica and I arrived, people were sitting around talking about politics and their college classes.

Local lawyers discussed protest laws and a political science professor spoke to us about tax law. After the question and answer period was over, a young woman went onstage. She was in her mid-twenties and had a pleasant face.

The young woman stood before the microphone holding pieces of paper and said, "Hi, I'm Ashley. I have a poem to read about our current situation. It's a poem by Sherwood Burke."

Monica and I looked at each other.

"Sherwood Burke? What the fuck?" I said.

"You think she knows where he is?"

"I don't know."

Onstage, Ashley continued. "Sherwood Burke sent me this poem to read here tonight. It's called 'You Really Killed the Buffalos for This?'"

She took a drink of coffee and said in a loud voice:

"I only have two justifications
for the death of capitalism
where did the Korean tiger and Buffalo go
I don't know
into capitalism's mouth and out
its fuckin' ass
I don't care
how good dental care is
and how much fun you have learning Bach on the violin
discussing Plato's Republic in an
air-conditioned building
because capitalism makes my dick hurt"

After the organized part of the meeting, Monica and I approached Ashley. She was sitting at a table talking to a few people. We introduced ourselves and I said, "I know Sherwood Burke. He was at NEOTAP, but he disappeared recently."

"I know," she said.

"You know what?"

"Sherwood and I were in the military together. We dated for a while. He sent me this poem in an email but he didn't say where he was. He just said to read the poem at local rallies for Protest 2.0. He didn't say anything else. I asked him why he wasn't in NEOTAP anymore but he didn't reply. I think he has a plan."

"A plan to do what?"

"I don't know," she said.

Under a Bed

I was doing the body count and could not find Armando Vasquez. I went from the lower-floor to the upper floor several times looking for Armando. I found Lawrence and asked if he'd seen Armando.

"No, but you better find him. Have you checked the passes? He might be out on work-release."

"Yes, I checked the work passes."

"Did you check the log book?"

"Yes."

"Well, look in every room. I'm sure he's here somewhere."

I was growing increasingly nervous. What if Armando escaped? What if Armando figured out how to break out of NEOTAP? If Armando escaped, Heidelberg would probably blame me because I did the body count. I considered just marking down his name but if he was really gone, my ass would be screwed.

I checked his room again. I looked under his bed this time. There was Armando.

I looked at him. He looked me.

He said nothing.

His eyes were ghost-like in the darkness under the bed.

I said, "Armando, get out of there."

"No."

I knew I was in deep shit. I was being tested. Heidelberg was somehow going to accuse me of not following procedure.

I said to Armando, "You seriously need to get out of there."

"No."

I was becoming really pissed.

"Armando, you need to get out from under there."

"...have politico problem..."

"What?"

"The case managers no help me. They only help me brain. No have a brain problem. Have politico problem."

I tried to remember the Spanish I'd learned in college. "Quieres ser escrito arriba?" My Spanish was for sure wrong.

"No, have a politico problem."

I needed to get him out from under the bed, but I wasn't allowed to talk to the residents because I was not properly trained in dealing with my fellow human beings. I said fuck it and asked, "What is your problem?"

"Have politico problem."

"I can't fix those problems."

"You no fix anything."

"If I have to get Imad, you will be in a lot of trouble."

I stood up and paced around the room. I knew this was bad. I was failing as a guard. I couldn't even get a resident out from under his bed. Heidelberg was going to fire me. I was never going to get health care and become an adult. I was going to have to go back to working at restaurants and my parents and grandfather would be disappointed in me. I looked under the bed again and no one was there.

"Armando!"

Armando wasn't there.

I found Lawrence and told him Armando disappeared.

"Go tell Imad," Lawrence said.

I went to Imad's office and closed the door. I said to Imad, "Armando disappeared."

Imad looked at me. He didn't have a facial expression. He listened like I was explaining something that didn't matter to him.

Finally, he said, "Okay, I'll fix it."

"Where did he go? How does someone disappear?"

Imad said, "Don't worry, I'll fix it."

I left the office. Armando disappeared and no one cared. I saw Imad leave his office and walk to Heidelberg's office. No one rushed around. Everyone moved without purpose, without a sense of urgency. A human had disappeared and no one cared. What kind of job did I have? After an hour passed, I checked the log book as well as the resident profiles and Armando was gone. There was no evidence of his existence anywhere in NEOTAP.

Edward Choffin

I was handing out mail and Imad came up to me. "Edward Choffin wants to see you." I stood there terrified. I knew I was going to get fired. The incident earlier in the morning with Armando was going to be too much to handle. I knew I had fucked it up.

A total sense of dread and anxiety came over me. I did not want to look at Edward Choffin. I did not want to hear him. I did not want to go near that man.

I walked into his office.

In the 1950s he would have had a bottle of scotch in the room. He would have poured me a drink and we would have lit up cigarettes. But this was 2011 and there was no scotch and no cigarettes. There was a fat guy in his fifties and a young guy who wanted to keep his job.

I must have looked horrible. I was sweating and felt about ready to cry.

Choffin looked at me and said, "Today you witnessed something unusual. You probably have questions about it. But you aren't allowed to ask any questions about it, so I will answer your questions, but you aren't allowed to ask any. I know what you are allowed to ask and not allowed to ask, so I will answer the questions you are allowed to ask, as long as you don't ask any questions.

"The government provides two main things to society. It provides the control of violence and it provides laws. How laws are made and if they make sense are not our concern at NEOTAP. NEOTAP's concern is the control of violence, the control of people who break laws. I don't care if the law makes sense or doesn't make sense, I don't even care what the laws are. What we must control at NEOTAP are the humans who break the law. To control humans is not easy. It's not an easy job we have at NEOTAP. To fulfill your duties, to control humans, you must believe not only in the law, but in NEOTAP. I'm starting to think that you don't believe in NEOTAP, Michael."

I didn't want to lose my job, so I said, "I have not lost faith. I was trying to understand NEOTAP better. It is obvious to me that in the context of modern America NEOTAP is the best possible outlet for criminals to be reformed. I would not under any circumstance prescribe alternative avenues for criminals to be reformed."

"Good, then we are agreed. The law is not written but authority."

"Yes, I completely agree."

I walked out of the office. As I walked down the hall, I realized that he never explained where Armando went.

Meeting Monica's Dad

Monica's dad said I needed to come over and help him rake leaves. Monica said it was very important to her dad that a family raked leaves together. She said her father believed that since the trees made the whole family happy by providing fruit and shade, it was a family's responsibility to pick up the leaves together.

I parked in front of her house and her dad was standing in the yard. He came over and shook my hand and said, "You must be Michael."

I shook his hand. His grasp was firmer than mine.

He told me his name was Milton.

Monica told me that her dad had worked at the same factory for twenty-two years making plastic parts for automobiles. He worked a forty hour shift five days a week. He had raised Monica alone. Monica hadn't seen her mother in years and hardly ever mentioned her.

We went into the kitchen and Milton said, "Would you like some apple cider?"

"Okay."

He poured two glasses of apple cider and said, "I believe

in the seasons. In the fall I drink apple cider and eat pumpkin pie. In the winter I drink eggnog and hot chocolate, and I eat soup. In the spring I watch the rain and grow my seedlings. In the summer I eat hot dogs and drink fresh-squeezed lemonade and watch my garden grow." He said it with a sense of pride, like he was in touch with the earth's shakings and grumblings.

"Do you want to see my Malibu?"

I realized he was talking about cars and said, "Sounds good."

We went into his garage and looked at his car. "This is a 1977 Malibu. When I got this car it was nothing but rust sitting in a junkyard. Now look at it. I take it down in the summer to the drag strip. Monica helped a lot in putting it together."

I stared at the car. It was burgundy, and it had giant tires with chrome hubcaps. Milton got in the car and started it up. It made a horrible rumbling sound. He got out of the car and came over to me and said, "Sounds awesome, doesn't it?"

"Yeah."

"This thing is fast, oh my god."

Monica came out all smiles, then we raked the lawn. Monica and Milton worked well together. They acted more like brother and sister than father and daughter.

After raking, we went inside and drank more apple cider. Milton said he was going to visit a friend for a few hours and we could have the house to ourselves.

Monica and I went to her bedroom to watch Netflix. We put on a Korean television show called *Boys Over Flowers*.

We began to kiss. The kisses were soft and sometimes I would kiss her cheek and sometimes she would kiss my closed eyes. We kept laughing the whole time. Monica took the remote and put the Korean drama on pause.

Slowly we started taking off each layer of clothing. First came shirts, then bra, then pants and underwear. It felt like years it took so long, but at the same time it felt like no time passed at all.

I ran my hands over her firm belly and groped her thighs. I kissed her thighs and belly. I ran my hands over her back and she ran her hands over mine. We smiled and said nothing. We were just two people having sex on a Thursday in America.

Both of us were inexperienced lovers. When I did a count, I think I'd had sex with a total of five people. Monica told me that she'd only had sex with three. Neither of us had ever been in a long-term relationship. We had both dated people for a year at most.

We lay there in bed afterwards and she turned the Korean drama back on.

I said, "I think you are wonderful."

She smiled and said, "I wanted you to meet my father before we had sex."

I laughed and said, "Why?"

"Because I wanted to know if he liked you. My father was here before you and he will be here after you."

"If you ever meet my parents you will laugh. They are not like your father."

"I don't expect them to be."

We finished watching the Korean drama. I cuddled her and we went to sleep.

Group Counseling

I was to be trained in group counseling. To better understand what the residents had to live through on a day to day basis I had to attend several workshops. The first workshop was Drug Counseling with Larry the case manager. Larry had worked for NEOTAP for thirteen years and never got tired of it. He seemed like a really nice guy. Many of the employees who had been there for more than ten years seemed really nice. They didn't have power complexes. I had heard through people who had worked there that several years ago Heidelberg was not in charge and things were different then.

Larry brought me into this office and sat me down. He said, "Now Michael, this drug counseling is very different, just four people are in it. They have been selected specifically because they are middle-class kids who went to college or are in college but can't get their lives together. It seems that they don't want college to end. They didn't grow up in poverty, they weren't abused when they were little, and they come from good families. We find that the middle-class kids and the poor kids don't resort to drugs for the same reasons, so having them in the same group seems like more of a conflict than a solution."

Larry brought me into a small room with windows where the group counseling took place. The three residents were already sitting there. I took a seat among them.

Larry sat down and said, "Okay, we are going to talk about how drugs make us feel today. I want you guys to be honest. No lies, just be honest. Okay, Tim, you go first."

Tim said, "From the ages of twelve to the present I have done drugs regularly, with some breaks in between. I've done alcohol, marijuana, cocaine, amphetamines, acid, ecstasy, mushrooms, Xanax, Oxycontin, heroin, nitrous oxide, ketamine, ether, morphine, and crack cocaine. I think of drugs as a good thing. To me, they are part of a diet. There is nothing different about food, sleep, exercise, what kind of books and music you like, the people you spend time with, and drugs. I mean, some people have no personality and do drugs to replace having to have a personality. But I still like drugs. So I don't know. It's all part of the fun of trying to kill yourself slowly and make it look like you're not trying, I guess. It's just a way to spend time."

Gin and Capri looked like they didn't care about a single thing he said. Alex Guevera looked like he wanted to cry. They were all staring into space, thinking their own thoughts.

Larry said, "Drugs are not part of a diet."

Tim didn't respond.

Larry said, "Now it's your turn, Alex."

Alex kept fiddling with a pencil in a nervous manner. After he was done fiddling with the pencil he would make paper footballs with paper from his notebook. His whole life seemed like a giant nervous spell. He looked around to make sure it was his turn. He could never quite figure when it was his turn to do something. "I used to use drugs to help me in different situations – Adderall for work, Xanax for sleep, painkillers for pain, you know – but now it's gotten to the point where I'll just do anything and everything I can get my hands on at any given moment simply for the sake of getting fucked up and forgetting what a shitty life I live. I know some people would say that I don't have it that bad but that's just what some people would say I guess. People say retarded shit, you know? I didn't start fucking with drugs like coke or molly or heroin until I started chilling with people who fucked with them and I liked them a little I guess, but I still think prescription shit is my favorite. Plus the high is consistent. I use Adderall, Xanax, marijuana, cigarettes and usually some type of painkiller – Promethazine-Codeine syrup and Percocet are my favorites – on a daily basis. Drinking's not really my thing. My friends and family say that drugs'll kill me but I honestly feel like...I mean...I know...like...it's a fact...that if it's not the drugs it'll be something else. A car crash, cancer, whatever. And I guess I'd just rather die high to be honest."

Larry looked at him with confusion and said, "What the hell is Promethazine?"

Gin said, "Yeah, what the hell is that?"

Alex started laughing and said, "Cough syrup. Some people call it lean, sizzurp, purple drank...shit makes you feel like you're floating in slow motion and shit."

The residents all began laughing.

Larry didn't laugh. He responded, "Getting high off cough syrup is dangerous. Responsible people do not get high off of cough syrup. You are in college, you have a bright future ahead of you but instead you are screwing around, ruining it. You are going to end up dropping out and having to work in a dishtank. There are millions of people who would love your opportunity and you're throwing it away on drugs."

We all sat there quiet.

Larry said, "Go ahead, Gin."

Gin sat there for a long time. He would smile for a few seconds and then stop, smile for a few second and then stop. Then he finally started talking. "I began using Adderall in college. The first time I used it I felt like I could barely walk because everything was so bright and new-looking. I was in the library working on an essay about the 9/11 conspiracy and I typed eighteen pages in three hours. I got a C- because my professor didn't believe in the conspiracy. If he just would watch any of the YouTube videos about WTC7...the most-watched result for a search of 9/11 on YouTube is a video that shows that the government definitely blew up both of the main towers. I don't think the masses can do anything anymore even if the government admitted they helped blow up the buildings. JFK was assassinated by the CIA and I don't think anything will happen to the CIA or the government at all before they all die. The same will happen with 9/11 and anything else from now on, I think. Maybe if the masses enacted some kind of guerilla warfare and began assassinating high-level officials and made a list of the richest five-hundred people and made it a goal to assassinate all of them, then maybe that could solve something."

We sat there confused by what he said. What did any of that have to do with drugs?

Larry said, "Okay, enough of the government conspiracies. Gin, you'll be written up for that. Capri, do you have something to say?"

Capri was a skinny little Italian guy with dark curly hair and sad eyes. Capri bit his fingernails constantly. Sometimes he would chew the nails so far down that he couldn't bite them, then he would gnaw the skin. I'd had to get him bandages for his bloody fingertips several times.

He didn't want to be in NEOTAP but like the rest of these middle-class young men, it kind of looked like he didn't want to be anywhere. Capri said, "I guess doing drugs is a really good way to accent boredom. It's a really good way to make friends. It's really difficult to have friends without drugs. Thinking about holding a coherent sober conversation still alarms me. I made friends for the first time in college, and I made these friends because we were all interested in the same brand of fun. Fun involving drugs. Fun involving getting drugs, doing drugs, talking about drugs. When there were no drugs we would drink until drugs were available again. We drank regardless. We drank endlessly. It was fun. People who like drugs always find each other, but I like to think I found the best ones. I haven't found a drug yet that rids me of anxiety. But there are many that cause me not to care about it. It feels really good. Even the drugs that make me anxious. I like them because I like to challenge myself. Sometimes drugs make work bearable. I went to work at a grocery store during the tail-end of an acid trip once and it was shitty. But now I know that I'm capable of doing it. Doing key-bumps in my car on my cigarette breaks felt like something between recklessness and practicality. It just feels neutral. It feels like maintenance. I've always worked really boring, mind-numbing, minimum wage jobs. Of course, they always made me feel anxious. It's good to have something to look forward to when your shift is over. Some people feed their dog and watch ESPN. Some people play drinking games with their friends and then go to a bar. Some people have sex with their significant other and then check different websites. Some people order Chinese food and read about philosophy. It's not that these activities are uninteresting to drug users. It's just...I would prefer to swallow something or smoke something or snort something before doing any of those things. Sometimes being high just feels a lot safer than the alternative. Sometimes being high just feels really comfortable."

I sat there and listened to Capri. It wasn't my life but I could see how someone else might view drugs as something that gives life meaning. I wanted to tell them they were nice people, and praise their honesty, but that was not how counseling at NEOTAP worked.

Visiting Lawrence

Monica and I were sitting outside Starbucks, drinking lattes. The sky was a nice pleasant shade of blue. Little white clouds dangled in the sky. The leaves were changing colors. Cars kept passing by.

"Lawrence lives nearby. We should go see him," Monica said.

"Why? He's insane."

"He might know why people are disappearing."

"He's only a shift supervisor," I said.

"He has the authority to pass out meds."

"Yeah, but passing out meds doesn't mean he knows why people are disappearing."

"We should go see him anyway," she said.

"Should we call him before we go over?"

"No, let's surprise him."

"He is totally a work douche."

"Oh god, I know. He came up to me the other day and said, 'I'm so proud to be working for NEOTAP. Sometimes when I wake up, I just can't wait to be here.'"

"What did you say?"

"Sounds good, Lawrence."

"What did he say?"

"Nothing, he just walked away smiling."

"So why do you want to visit him?"

"I don't know," she said.

We got into Monica's Honda Civic and drove over to Lawrence's house. The house he lived in was small. It was nothing to be proud of.

We walked up to the door and knocked. A man – maybe a friend, maybe a roommate, maybe Lawrence's brother – came to the door. He was in his mid-thirties and didn't look like a serious person. He was wearing jogging pants and a ripped New England Patriots jersey. We looked at him standing there in his New England Patriots jersey. He looked at us and said, "Hi."

"Is Lawrence here?" I asked.

"Yeah, I guess."

"Can we talk to him?"

"If you want," the man said in a sad monotone voice.

The man led us into the house, which was messy. It didn't smell bad, but there were clothes piled up in a corner, magazines and newspapers in tumbling stacks, and the furniture looked old and dirty. There were barely any pictures on the walls. It didn't look like a happy place to live. The word 'pathetic' occurred to me.

The man knocked on Lawrence's door and said, "Hey Lawrence, there are some people here for you."

"What!" Lawrence screamed from the bedroom.

"People, Lawrence, people."

"Who are they?"

He looked at us and said, "Who are you?"

"Tell him it's Monica and Mike from work," Monica said.

"Monica and Mike from work."

Lawrence yelled back, "NEOTAP employees can't talk to other NEOTAP employees outside of work. It's against the rules."

Monica said, "Tell him we just want to talk for a minute."

"They just want to talk to you for a minute, goddamn it. Open the fucking door. What the fuck is wrong with you?"

Lawrence opened the door. We stared at Lawrence and he stared at us. He looked insane.

Lawrence waved us into his room.

Lawrence's room looked like the room of a fourteen-year-old boy. There were posters of women in bikinis on the wall, several football trophies from the early 2000s, a twin bed, clothes scattered on the floor, and virtually nothing that signified an adult male lived in the room.

Lawrence sat on the bed and said, "Hi guys."

We stood in the room. There were no chairs and the floor was too covered in clothes to sit down.

"Lawrence, do you know where people go when they disappear?" Monica said.

"Disappear from where?"

"From NEOTAP."

"I don't know what you're talking about."

Monica responded forcefully. "Lawrence, I know you know what I'm talking about. You know that Sherwood Burke and several others have disappeared. Even Jay Riddick disappeared and he was an employee. Where did they go?"

Lawrence put his hands over his face and said, "I don't know what you are talking about."

I stood there. I didn't know what to say. I wasn't an aggressive person but Monica was. She continued, "Lawrence, quit fucking around. At least admit that you know people are disappearing."

Lawrence got into the fetal position on the bed, then he started to cry a little. "Heidelberg would kill me. Heidelberg, Heidelberg, Heidelberg, she brings me into her office every week and tells me I'm doing a horrible job, she hates me, she hates me, she walks by me and whispers to me that I'm doing everything wrong, then she gives me a raise and even a promotion but she doesn't say why, she keeps telling me I'm doing a horrible job. She brought me into the office yesterday and told me I didn't know how to take care of the residents, she told me I didn't know how to run the cafeteria, I thought I was good at running the cafeteria, she told me I needed to yell more at the residents, then she told me two hours later never to yell at the residents, I don't know, I don't understand anything, I've worked twenty-two days in a row, this is my first day off in twenty-two days, but I can't stop thinking about Heidelberg, I can never stop thinking about Heidelberg. All I wanted to be growing up was a cop, but they aren't hiring, so I stay at NEOTAP. I am so afraid of Heidelberg, I am so much more afraid of Heidelberg than you."

We stood there.

"Maybe we can help you," Monica said.

"You can't help me!" Lawrence screamed, still lying in the fetal position, crying.

I asked him, "Why don't you just quit?"

"I'm afraid of Heidelberg."

"If you get another job, Heidelberg won't be there," I said.

"Heidelberg is everywhere, she sees everything."

"That is insane," Monica said.

"Lawrence, why won't you tell us where people go?" I said.

"I don't know where they go. I don't know. I asked once and they told me I wasn't allowed to ask that question, so I never asked again."

Monica and I looked at each other, disappointed. I said, "Lawrence, we're going to leave now, okay?"

"You better leave before Heidelberg finds you here. She might have the room bugged."

"Why would you think she has your room bugged?" Monica said.

"One time she came up to me and said, 'I know you were talking shit about me to a girl on the phone.' Then she walked away."

"Was it true?" I asked.

"Yeah, I was trying to date a girl, and I talked shit about Heidelberg while on the phone with her."

Monica said, "Holy shit, Heidelberg has the power to bug phones?"

"Let's go," I said, "before we get Lawrence into trouble."

We didn't say bye to Lawrence. All he wanted was for us to leave anyway.

We got into Monica's car and I said, "I think this is Stockholm Syndrome."

"What the fuck is that?"

"I learned about it in college. It's when a hostage has compassion for their kidnapper, but it can work with bosses and employees. A boss is terribly cruel ninety percent of the time but ten percent of the time gives them little things like raises and promotions to keep them thinking that the boss actually loves them and is being cruel to them for their own good."

"Oh god, that is NEOTAP, that is Heidelberg."

"Yeah, that is totally Heidelberg."

"Yeah, but how does Heidelberg have the power to bug Lawrence's phone?"

"I don't know. Maybe NEOTAP isn't just NEOTAP. Maybe it's connected to something bigger like the CIA or FBI."

"Oh man, this is screwed up," Monica said.

We talked for hours trying to figure it all out. We went back on the NEOTAP website and looked up Heidelberg's profile but it said nothing about having the power to wiretap people. Then we wondered if Lawrence would snitch on us for asking him about the disappearing people. I started to feel stressed out. Nothing made any sense. I felt like I was soon going to be gone myself.

Dental Hygiene

I had to sign in Clinton Walker after he came back from the dentist. Clinton Walker was an obese man with an ugly face. We sat at a small round table across from each other. I had to sign several papers and date them. It was essential that documentation was perfect. If documentation was inaccurate I would have to visit Heidelberg and get scolded. I looked at Clinton Walker. His face was pockmarked. His nose was too big. His skin was alabaster and sickly looking.

"What happened at the dentist?"

"They took two teeth out."

"What was wrong with them?"

"They were rotted."

"How did they get them out."

"They just pulled them?"

"Damn."

"I have to go back next week to get some more pulled."

"Damn."

Then he looked right at me and said, "I know you hate this place. I know that everyone who acts like you disappears, gets fired, who the fuck knows, so I will tell you the truth about what NEOTAP has taught me, because I know you won't tell."

Suddenly Imad appeared. "I'll take this from here. Go search lockers," he told me.

I had Clinton Walker sign the last few pages detailing his dental visit and Imad took him away.

Searching Lockers

I put on a pair of gloves and got a list of lockers that needed to be searched. Searching lockers was boring but for some reason I liked it a lot. I liked looking at the residents' stuff, seeing what they were reading, looking through their notebooks.

I went into a room and opened a locker; I looked through their socks, put my hand into their shirts and pants, skimmed their notebooks and found a newspaper clipping reporting that Lester Wallace's brother had died of a drug overdose. I thought about Lester Wallace. He could barely read. He got into trouble constantly for being a slow eater in the cafeteria. He couldn't get along with the other residents. I checked the rest of Lester's locker and found five magazines. I called for him over the walkie-talkie.

Lester Wallace came into the room. He stood there, a small, fragile man. I said, "Lester, you have five magazines. You can only have two."

"I ain't got no idea where they came from."

"But Lester, this is your locker. You have to know where they came from. Somebody must have given you these magazines."

"No, I don't know."

"But these magazines are in your locker."

"I ain't put no magazines in my locker."

"Then where did they come from?"

"I don't know," he said.

"Listen, if you don't admit that these are your magazines then I will have to write you up. Do you want that?"

"No."

"Okay then, how did you get these magazines?"

"I don't know, they ain't mine."

"Okay, I am going to write you up and put these magazines in storage."

"You can throw them away."

"Why would I throw them away?"

"I don't know."

He looked confused. He didn't want to admit to anything. I bet if I'd asked him if he existed, he would have told me he didn't.

"Okay Lester, go join the others."

"Seriously, I ain't got no idea where those magazines came from. Somebody must've put them in my locker."

"To frame you?" I said.

"Yeah, something like that. I ain't got no five magazines."

"Seriously?"

"Man, you setting me up for the woo."

"What the hell does that mean?"

"That means you setting me up to get into trouble. You itching to write me up."

"Okay, I'm going to write you up. Now get out of here."

"Whatever."

Lester Wallace left the room.

PART TWO

Troubleshooting

Monica walked into NEOTAP. She went into the office and said hi to Lawrence and Imad. She didn't know Imad and Lawrence like Mike did. She didn't have to interact with them on a power basis. She would say hi to everyone, have small talk about sports, computers, or random life things. Everyone knew that Monica loved Arby's and would eat Arby's at least three times a week. Sometimes people called her Arby's Girl.

Monica had been to work for an hour and she had not seen Mike. She took a walk out to where the residents were but she didn't see him. She asked Lawrence, "Where's Mike?"

"I don't know," Lawrence said.

"Did he call in sick?"

"No."

Monica considered herself a troubleshooter. Her life was about fixing problems. Her dad had taught her the joy of solving problems. When something broke, they fixed it together. When the car broke, they fixed it together. When the roof leaked, they fixed it together. When the water heater needed to be replaced, they took it out and replaced it together.

When Monica got her first computer, she fell in love. She was twelve and learned all about HTML code and Run and all the strange things only computer geeks care about.

She wanted to solve the problem of Mike's whereabouts. She kept asking people. She went into Heidelberg's office and asked, "Where's Mike? He should be here by now."

Heidelberg looked at her and said, "Shouldn't you be updating files or something?"

Monica focused on machines so much because she actually didn't like people and their rudeness and to Heidelberg she responded, "No, I should be looking for Mike."

"Get out of my office," Heidelberg said.

"You can't even tell me if he called off?"

"You aren't allowed to ask that question."

Monica considered ripping Heidelberg's face off but decided to leave the office.

She walked by the employee mailboxes. Mike's name was gone. She checked the schedule and his name was gone. She returned to her office and looked up Mike in the NEOTAP database and his name was gone from there as well.

She texted Mike, she called him twenty times, she called his grandfather and then his parents, but still nothing. No one knew where Mike was.

Mike had disappeared.

She sat in her office thinking about Mike. She thought about how he listened to her when she talked. How he listened for hours one night to her talking about working on cars with her dad. How Mike allowed her to fix the headlight on his car. How Mike made her laugh when she was sad. She also thought about having sex with Mike. She had grown fond of him, had begun to fall in love with him. She didn't know about babies or getting a house in the suburbs, but she wanted to be with him. He seemed like a good guy. College-educated, presentable, courteous.

She packed up and left. She knew it was only a matter of time before she disappeared too. It was over for her.

Monica stopped by Mike's house, hoping maybe there was something in his NEOTAP handbook that would direct her to where he'd gone.

Mike's grandpa was sitting at the kitchen table. He was drinking coffee and reading the newspaper. He looked up at her and said, "Monica, have you heard from Mike?"

"No, have you?"

"No."

"I think he disappeared."

"What does that even mean – disappear? How does one disappear?"

"I don't know, but people do at NEOTAP, they just disappear."

"The government is the alpha and omega, the first and the last, the beginning and the end. Remember that."

Monica nodded. "I am coming to find that out. It didn't really bother me that people were disappearing when it was people I didn't know, but now it's personal."

Monica went into Mike's room. Mike's NEOTAP handbook was on the floor. She read through it page by page, but it never mentioned anyone disappearing.

Monica considered people to call. She thought of Choffin. She called him on her cellphone.

"Hello?" Choffin said.

"Yes, this is Monica."

"Oh hi Monica. What would you like?"

"Where is Mike? He wasn't at work today."

"Mike? Mike who?"

"Michael Scipio."

"I don't know any Michael Scipio."

"But he's worked for NEOTAP for months."

"I don't really talk to employees."

"Okay, where is Sherwood Burke, Armando, and the others?"

"I don't know them either. I can't recall any of those names."

"None?"

"None."

"Okay, goodbye."

Monica ended the call.

She lay down on Mike's bed, put her head on his pillow. It smelled like him. She could smell him a little.

She looked through the pile of NEOTAP materials again. She noticed there was a book called *Reality Conversion* by Dr. Charles Nevitsky. Monica remembered that Nevitsky had written the program for NEOTAP. He was the mastermind behind NEOTAP. If anyone had any idea why people were disappearing, it would be Nevitsky.

Monica went online and Googled Dr. Charles Nevitsky. Over sixty thousand pages turned up on him. He was considered one of the great minds of the 20th Century. You couldn't graduate with a psychology degree without having to write at least one paper on him. He was the first person to take the works of Skinner and European Existentialism and combine them into one psychology – cognitive behavioral therapy. She read that he was still alive, living less than two hours away. She became excited, but also filled with anxiety. She thought it was a stupid lead but she had to do something. She kept thinking that it all seemed stupid. Why would

NEOTAP make one of its own employees disappear? Why would the world of humans create buildings where people get treated like shit and if they have an opinion about how shitty they are being treated, they make them disappear?

She went into the kitchen and found the old man sitting there. He looked sad. "Do you have a gun?" Monica asked.

"Yeah, why?"

"I think I might need it to get Michael back."

"Do you know how to shoot a gun?"

"Yes, my dad taught me. He would take me out to the woods and we would shoot pop cans. I wasn't a bad shot."

"Listen to me. Don't forget to have fun."

Monica was surprised. "How can this be fun?"

"You won't find him unless you are having fun. Remember that the assholes who took him, the assholes who run this world, are having loads of fun being big and powerful, being assholes. You won't defeat them unless you love this, unless you are also having fun, unless you are having more fun than them."

Monica stood there. She had never thought about hunting down a fellow human, and she never thought of it as being fun. Then she remembered Benny Baradat in the coffee shop talking about fun. She wondered why all these crazy white men were talking about fun in the face of all these shitty things.

The old man walked into the living room and she followed him. He pulled a handgun, a small black revolver, from a chest. He held the gun along with some bullets. "Take it," he said.

Monica held out her small hand and he placed the gun there. Then he pulled out a shoulder holster and said, "Put it on."

Monica took off her coat and put it on. She fixed the straps so it fit nicely. She practiced taking out the gun a couple of times. She smiled and felt powerful holding the gun. She wanted Mike back. She wanted to end NEOTAP and all its stupid shit. She even wanted crazy Sherwood Burke back and all the criminals from NEOTAP. She started to feel strong and confident with the gun so close to heart.

She told the old man, "I will find him."

"I know, because you have to," he said.

Monica left.

The old man sat down at the kitchen table. He had read history books and knew the power of governments, and he felt scared for Monica.

Monica drove to her house to see her father and pick up a few things. She went inside the house. She felt strange looking at it. She felt like it might be the last time she ever looked at the house. It made her look deeper at the pictures of her and her father standing by the ocean. Everything seemed more real, full of color, the couch, the kitchen, even the bathtub, all the objects in the house were full of memories.

She came out of her bedroom carrying a backpack. Her father, sitting on a recliner watching television, said, "Where you off to, Monica?"

"On a little vacation."

"How come you never told me about it?"

"It just came up. It's only for four days. Going to Chicago." She thought Chicago sounded nice. Chicago was her favorite place to go for a few days at a time.

"Oh, well give me a hug."

She knew that every time she went on vacation, they would tell each other 'I love you.' This would give her a perfect chance to do so without revealing her true plans.

They hugged and told each other 'I love you.' She hugged her father for an unusually long time. After she walked out the door, she began to cry.

Dr. Charles Nevitsky

Monica experienced terrible anxiety while driving to Nevitsky's house. She pulled the car into a gas station parking lot. She opened her purse and took out a Xanax and an Adderall and swallowed them both at once. She liked the feel of the Adderall pumping her up. Adderall made her excited, gave her powerful feelings of confidence. She would take the Xanax to calm the anxiety caused by the Adderall. She had never told anyone that she regularly took pills to feel good. Mike knew and took them sometimes with her, but mostly she kept it a secret.

Monica felt that pills made life exciting. It was exciting to troubleshoot on a computer, it was exciting to have sex, it was exciting to take a hike in the woods. But it did not make her body feel excited. She considered pills a little vacation for her body.

She decided that to do this whole thing, to find Mike, she needed drugs. She wasn't going to be able to be confident and strong without drugs. She knew that without drugs she was a timid little girl who just wanted to play on her computer. She knew the situation required her to live up to the task.

Monica arrived at Dr. Charles Nevitsky's house. It was a large two-story house. It was old but well-kept. She looked at his house, afraid, but she wanted to find Michael, wanted to hold Michael again. She liked cuddling Michael at night and she didn't want that to disappear from her life.

She knocked on the door.

She waited.

The door opened.

An old man stood there, feeble and sad. He was bald, had red blotchy skin and long bushy eyebrows that stuck straight out. He looked professional though. He had on a nice shirt and nice pants. He still had grace and composure. He was elegant, he was strong, a man to be feared.

Monica looked at him and he looked at her.

Nevitsky said to Monica, "What would you like?"

Monica's Adderall had kicked in and she felt awesome. She said, "I need to find my man."

"Come in," he said.

They walked into the living room. Nevitsky walked slowly, limping a little from brain cancer he'd had several years ago. Nevitsky had not changed his habits from his youth. He knew negotiations required liquor. Nevitsky poured some scotch and said, "What do you drink? I don't think your generation drinks scotch, no?"

"Do you have any spiced rum?"

"Spiced rum. What a generation."

Nevitsky found some spiced rum and poured her a glass. He handed it to Monica and said, "So what is the problem?" He sat down, took on an active listening pose.

"I work at a place called NEOTAP. NEOTAP is a government treatment center for criminals. Well, I work IT, but my boyfriend works as a guard and, like, now he's disappeared. And some of the prisoners have also disappeared. So has another employee."

"But what does it have to do with me?"

"Well, the place is based on your book *Reality Conversion*."

Nevitsky sat there thinking, trying to remember writing *Reality Conversion*, why he wrote it, what was going on in his life when he wrote it, what that book meant to his life. Finally he said, "They are still using that book?"

"Yes."

"My god, that book was written to defeat the Soviets. The Soviets have been gone for twenty years. There is no reason to use that book anymore."

"What? I don't understand," Monica said, confused.

Dr. Charles Nevitsky, besides being a psychologist, was a professor for a good portion of his life. He was a man who liked to talk, but he hadn't had an audience in over ten years. Everyone had forgotten him and how he was a great psychologist. Sometimes a student writing a doctoral thesis would come by and ask him a few questions, but that was becoming rarer as the years passed. He grew excited to talk. This girl looked like one of his students from the past: young, pretty, and full of life.

Dr. Charles Nevitsky began to talk, "*Reality Conversion* was written in the late fifties by request of Eisenhower. Eisenhower requested a secret commission, an elite group of psychologists, scientists, political scientists, philosophers, geologists, geographers, theologians, historians and even a few novelists and marketing men. Our meetings took place in CIA headquarters. We all got a letter from the CIA stating that if we participated, we would receive a yearly sum of money and a wonderful pension, so we went. It was a wonderful event to me. The room was full of the best people America had to offer. It felt like I was in ancient Athens or Florence during the Renaissance. It made me so happy to be in that room with those extraordinary people.

"We all sat at a roundtable in a very efficient room. Allen Dulles, the head of the CIA, came in the room. I was very impressed by him and felt nervous to be in his presence. I was thirty years old then and was still starting my career, and still nervous about such things. Allen Dulles told us that we needed to defeat the Soviets, but there was a problem of belief that was coming. He stated that God had died and there was nothing that could produce a feeling of security and motivation in the lives of men. He stated that he had traveled the world and knew history, that the comfort of religion was vital to man's happiness and his will to do his duty to his country. He said that America needed a religion that would make the people do their duty and be strong, confident Americans, which meant going to work, rearing their children and not becoming communists. The most important thing was not becoming communists.

"We all agreed that this was vital to America. He gave us a year to do research on the project. He said the government would give us all the money we wanted for our research. The government was handing us a blank check. On top of everything else, we received free housing.

"After a year, we presented our research to Allen Dulles. We knew the most enduring religion was Islam, and what was Islam founded on? Five simple pillars. It's basically belief in one God, prayer, tithing, visiting Mecca, and fasting. These things are simple. No need to even think about them. So we tried to emulate that, and this is what we came up with. One: Go to work and do your job. Two: Care for your children. Three: Pay your bills. Four: Obey the law.

Five: Buy products. These were simple rules to follow and we could notify all citizens of these rules through television, movies, literature and commercials. Allen Dulles loved it. Eisenhower loved it. Of course, there were objections. I told them that this was materialism. This was what the Soviets were doing. They make people into things. They didn't let people live and become what they wanted. A geologist argued that we needed to incorporate environmental values into the new religion. A philosopher stated that this method was too rigid and that we would become a decadent civilization. The novelist, to our surprise, said that America has had extraordinary people since its founding, that the country only invites the extraordinary, and this method of living would turn people into television-watching consumer automatons, that our children would become weak in mind. He said that we might become complacent, that established paradigms and procedures ranging from government to novels to how we run businesses would not be changed, there would be no innovation, bureaucracy would contaminate everything, that people should run the procedures and not the other way around. That innovation would be destroyed.

"Dulles looked at us and said that we were fighting the communists, that the communists had no problem killing twenty million of their own people, that if communists took control of America then twenty million people would die and live in gulags, and that we could sacrifice a little innovation for the sake of twenty million people not dying, and all of us in this room not being locked away in a gulag. He said this program would end after we beat the Soviets, that after we beat the Soviets we could return to a purer version of America. We did not ask what that was. We didn't even know what that meant.

"What was strange was that it came true, every one of our predictions except one. The geographer stated something strange but true. He said that nations are cultures that share the same language, but they are more culture than language and culture is derived from landscape. He said that the essence of culture was determined by the buildings people lived in, what they ate, how they worshipped, what music they listened to and what they talked about and that all things were derived from the landscape, that culture arose organically from the elements provided by the landscape that the humans were engulfed in. He brought out a map and said that every nation has become a nation because nature has blocked them in from the other groups. He cited islands, then nations blocked in by mountains, then he cited deep jungles and deserts. He then showed us how the weather in the south changed dramatically from the north, and then he showed us the mountains and deserts that separate parts of America from one another. He stated that America would have an unnatural culture if we forced everyone to believe in the same things, eat the same things, talk about the same things, listen to the same music and do the same things. That trying to keep people together through television and national media wasn't sustainable. He said that it would be very hard for America to sustain itself because geographically it shouldn't be one nation, that eventually when communication and when quick and easy travel broke down, there would be a division in culture. But he said that could take a hundred years and was not important when it came to defeating the Soviets.

"We defeated the Soviets. I don't know why anyone is still using that old paradigm. I figured they would have come up with a new one by now," Nevitsky concluded.

"But we aren't," Monica said, "it's still the same shit. The Soviets are gone but we're still fighting them."

"Oh, we aren't fighting the Soviets anymore. I could see when Reagan lowered taxes and deregulated the banks, the wealthy had the intelligence, as in CIA intelligence, to know the Soviets had lost and would disappear soon. There were no communists to fight anymore. Why not deregulate everything and destroy the unions? Capitalism and democracy had won, so we went crazy and did anything we wanted. But obviously that didn't work."

"But why are they still trying to control people with the old system?" said Monica.

"I suppose because there has been no *reason* to change it."

"A reason?"

"There are very few *reasons* given in life."

"Oh my god, you are nuts. Everyone is fucking nuts."

"No, listen. It might seem terrible and absurd, but if you look back, you'll see we had no choice. We needed to beat the Soviets. That was reason enough."

"But in the end you became the Soviets. We have a huge bureaucratic government and huge bureaucratic corporations. Even me, little me, all I wanted to do was work on computers and I ended up a bureaucrat."

Monica felt a terrible pain in her body. She wanted to shoot Nevitsky for creating The Five Pillars, she wanted to destroy everything, she wanted all the pain and fear to end, she wanted everything to be simple. She wanted her old life to come back. She wanted to sit with Mike at a coffee shop discussing the news and what movie they should watch on Netflix. She wanted everything to be normal. But she knew it was over. The normal would never return. She had seen things, she had thought thoughts, she had felt things that would never her allow to feel normal again.

Monica said, "So where is my boyfriend? You must know. You must have some connection at least."

"Maybe we have become our enemy. Maybe we studied them so hard, eventually we became them."

"I don't care about all these stories. I want to know where Michael is."

Nevitsky looked at her and said, "I will try to help."

He went into another room and made a phone call. Monica could hear him talking on the phone. She heard Nevitsky yell over the phone, "It doesn't matter. We've already lost. We finally lost to the Soviets. Just tell me you'll help."

Monica sat in the nicely decorated room with an old grand piano and black and white pictures of people long dead. She didn't understand Nevitsky. Nevitsky was a great man who conquered the world. He was a man with a long history of rewards and power. He had dined with famous people all over the world. Monica was just an awkward girl from some nameless town that no one cared about. She had an IT degree from a state university and had never won awards her whole life.

When Nevitsky reentered the room Monica said, "Why are you helping me? I'm just a little nothing of a human."

Nevitsky replied, "No, you aren't little. A little person would never bolt into my house demanding to know the truth. You may not be one of the elite, but you have the determination of a warrior, and the elite cannot exist without warriors."

"What is the news?" She felt terrible inside. She needed another Xanax. She felt out of control. She felt powerless.

The only thing keeping her together was the gun under her coat.

Nevitsky said, "I have someone who can help you. He knows the secret you are seeking. I didn't ask him what the secret was. I am too old to care about such things anymore."

Monica looked at Nevitsky and said, "Thank you."

Nevitsky handed her a piece of paper. "This man will be at this diner in this location at this time. Do not miss it. He will be wearing a cowboy hat. He's in his forties. Do not pull a gun on him. He is a trained CIA agent and will be able to disarm you and kill you so fast you won't even know that you died." Nevitsky paused. "I now end my life as a criminal. All my life I have fought against criminal behavior and now, in my last days, I will die a criminal."

"Maybe being a criminal isn't that bad after all," Monica said.

Dr. Charles Nevitsky poured himself another scotch, sat down in his favorite chair, and stared out the window at the wind blowing the colored leaves of the trees. He did not smile. He did not sigh. He just looked.

A Transmission from Burke

Monica was sitting at a Starbucks. She had stopped in some nameless town in Oklahoma to rest from driving and check her email. She felt depressed about leaving her father. She kept thinking of him walking around the house alone. She would often cook him meals, tuna fish and noodles, shit on a shingle, macaroni and cheese mixed with ground chuck. Then they would sit together and eat those meals talking about the days they'd had. She would wash his clothes and help him weed-whack the lawn because he had allergies and the weed-whacking made him sneeze a lot. She thought about all of his little habits, from drinking too much coffee to eating an excess of powdered donuts, to leaving barely any orange juice and milk left in the cartons and putting them back in the refrigerator anyway. She loved how he watched baseball games from beginning to end. Even though she did not love baseball, she would pretend she liked it so as not to upset him. She felt worried about him.

As she was sitting there, secluded in a sad daydream about her father, a woman sat across from her at the table. Monica realized she knew who she was. It was Ashley, the woman who read Sherwood Burke's poem at the Protest 2.0 meeting. Monica felt extremely confused and said, "Ashley?"

"Yes, from the meeting."

"Yeah," Monica said.

"I have a new email."

"Wait, how did you know I was here?"

"I have my sources."

"You have sources?"

"Yes, but so do you," Ashley said.

"Do we have the same sources?"

"No, but they're similar in form and function."

"Okay." Monica wanted to go back to daydreaming about her dad, but she knew that Ashley must have something to tell her, or she wouldn't have taken the time to find her in the middle of Oklahoma.

Ashley said, "I have a new email. It is Sherwood Burke's Talking Points."

"Burke has Talking Points?"

"Yes, in the past it would have been called a manifesto, an ideology, or even a treatise, but today ideas are called Talking Points."

"Show me the email."

Ashley took her laptop and went to her email and pulled up Burke's email and showed it to Monica. As Monica read, Ashley sipped on a chai and stared into space politely.

The Talking Points
of Sherwood Burke

I, Sherwood Burke, propose a new government, a new paradigm, a new mode of living that will make all Americans happy, I will give them what they want, because I am the Last True Democrat!

These facts were revealed to me and I consider them the most important facts:

1: People of the lower-uneducated-classes are having children at a higher rate than people from the middle to upper-educated-classes. The educated classes are only having babies at a .5 percent level but the people from the lower classes are having babies at an astounding 3.7 percent level, which implies that in thirty years the uneducated rabble of society will be the dominant majority in America. We must prepare a way for them to live!

2: Americans are fat. We must make a way for them to stop consuming disgusting food and not exercising.

3. The United States government spent sixty-six billion dollars on a plane called the Taradactle 24, which did not work, and there was zero demand for the production of the

aircraft. It was only made because a company gave campaign donations to politicians, which got them voted in, which led to the politicians voting in legislation to have it made. It was a sixty-six billion dollar scam. During this same time in legislative history the congress voted to decrease funding to the Center for Disease Control (CDC). The CDC performs a vital function. Our politicians are more concerned with their campaign donations than with the health of its citizens, therefore it is no longer a legitimate government.

WHAT WE NEED NOW

Destruction of quick and easy transportation by cars and trucks!

It will destroy nationwide corporations that depend on the highway system and the automobile. Without the automobile, states will be forced to be more isolated in their economic activities and will have to depend on their own resources and not the resources of other states and countries to survive. This will lead to the growth of local cultures and economies.

This will make everyone happy but the only way we can achieve this is by throwing off the chains of the automobile and the interstate highway system. The logic is sound. If we take away automobiles then Americans will be forced to become more local and more sustainable in their behaviors.

In thirty and especially in fifty years the educated class will become so small that they will need to become like the monks and nuns of the Dark Ages. The creation of the monasteries and convents in the Dark and Middle Ages was because the educated became so few after the collapse of the Roman Empire that they realized they were outnumbered and were not the majority. The majority was the rabble plowing the fields and slaughtering the goats. They realized that they did not matter.

This is the new plan, the new dream, we can still have democracy, checks and balances and a president, I don't care, but THE AUTOMOBILE MUST GO!

Monica read the Talking Points and said to Ashley, "This is fucking insane."

"It's logical."

"I guess so. But I like my car. I like cellphones and flat screen televisions."

"That's because you grew up that way, that's all. And you don't like those things, you feel comfortable around those things. There is a difference between 'liking' something and feeling 'comfortable' around something. A lot of older white people feel 'comfortable' when they don't see any black people working at a business or in their house. Does that make it right?"

"Are you saying I'm some sort of racist but in terms of my lifestyle, like I'm prejudiced against a world that doesn't have cellphones and flat screen televisions?"

"Yeah, you don't understand it, so you dismiss it."

"I don't know."

"We are comfortable being surrounded by gadgets and science but humans lived for thousands of years never having those things, and in those thousands of years we never had man-induced global warming or so much destruction to the environment and we never spent so little time with our families and neighbors. Before automobiles, government was very local, and people created the products they used, from clothes to plates and cups. We had a world of unique things that we made with our own hands. It was different before, and I believe better."

"But people died a lot earlier then?"

"Yes, but they lived a life where they created things. What is better: living a life creating things or working for some corporation pumping out plastic parts all day, or working in an office doing work for a company that doesn't care if you exist or not? What is better?"

"God, I don't know. I need to find Mike."

"Go find Mike and you'll see."

Monica picked up her latte and went out the door. She didn't say goodbye to Ashley. She thought of her father again and how much he loved his flat screen television.

The CIA Agent

Monica drove for a day and a night. The meeting place was a thousand miles away from Nevitsky's house. She couldn't stop thinking about Michael. She wanted him back so badly. She wanted to hold him, she wanted to laugh with him, she liked how he made her feel safe. She wanted to feel safe again. There didn't seem to be any safety left in the world. She wondered if she was doing the right thing. She doubted if trying to find Michael was the right thing to do. She doubted if it would make her life better. Monica considered the pros and cons. If she didn't find Michael, she could return home and get a job designing websites or doing IT for a large corporation. She could work hard for years and get promotions and maybe one day have enough money to have kids and get a house when she was like thirty-five. Maybe if she tried hard enough it would work. She was still young and pretty. She could find someone else to love, a man who wouldn't disappear.

She imagined that Michael was dead and it didn't matter. What if she found him and it was just a sad grave? What would she do then? She didn't know what to think.

Nothing in her life had prepared her to think about such things. In college they never trained her to troubleshoot her boyfriend disappearing because of political reasons. She kept thinking about what Nevitsky said, how we became Soviets. She realized that was probably a hint as to what kind of situation Michael was in, but she had never studied Soviet history. She knew the Soviets were the communist government of Russia from the beginning of the last century to the end of the century, but she didn't know the specifics. She realized that because she didn't know history she could not troubleshoot the situation. She didn't have the power to think about what was happening to her. She was ignorant. She decided that if she lived through this situation she would find out how all these things came together. Then it occurred to her that was why she and so many people are so easy to control: because they didn't know history. They couldn't place all these events together to make sense of their reality. She realized that her reality made no sense. That her mind couldn't make sense of what she was feeling. She was putting every effort into understanding what she was seeing and feeling, but she couldn't because she did not contain enough knowledge.

She realized she might die. The fear of death crept into her body and made her want to vomit. She had barely thought about her own death her entire life. She didn't like to think about death. She pulled over on the side of the road and took more Xanax and Adderall. She realized she had not slept in two days. She went into a gas station and bought a large coffee and sucked it down with donuts. She felt sick. The idea of dying kept coming back to her. Was it even worth it, dying for a man? Dying for love? Dying for good sex and laughs and a possible future with children and a nice house. But if she was dead, she would enjoy none of that. She became afraid. But she wanted Michael back. She wanted to hold him again. She realized she had a *reason*. For the first time in her life she had a *reason* to do something. Up to that point she had spent her life doing what she was told. She was told to go to school, she went. She was told to go to college, she went. She was told to get a job with health care, she did. She realized her whole life was founded on the Five Pillars. She was nothing but a little robot, controlled, a tame little animal. This thought screamed in her head. They had taken her power as a human. They had locked her out of her own power. Her power was there since she was born but the government and the media did everything they could to divert her away from her own power. Her own primitive power of feeling and poetry.

Monica had spent her life doing the logical thing, believing that if she did what she was told she would be rewarded, that if she kept her head down and charged ahead in life, life would give her what she wanted. But life had not given her what she wanted. It had actually taken what she wanted from her. She had taken pills her whole life to reduce this feeling, to make the anxiety go away, pop another Xanax and it will all go away. She decided not to take Xanax anymore, but she would still take Adderall. She wanted all the anxiety now, she wanted to feel it all, to be submerged in her feelings, into the poetry that blasts and beats, resounds and trumpets in her heart. She wanted to hear the war drums pounding in her soul. She felt so extreme, she wanted to scream. She wanted to smash everything and shoot cars driving by. She wanted to shoot herself. She considered pulling over on the side of the road and blowing her brains out. She imagined slowly stopping the car, putting the car in park, turning the car off, leaning back in the front seat, pulling the gun out of the holster, then putting the gun in her mouth and pulling the trigger. It would all be over, all the fear and anxiety, all the stupidity and absurdity, all the meaningless life she had lived and was forced to live. But she had to get Michael. She had to solve this problem. She punched the steering wheel, she began to cry, she popped another Adderall and screamed. She had to push ahead.

She felt scared to die. But it made sense now. Up to that car ride across America to find Michael, her life had not made sense. But there was a *reason* now for her life, for her behavior. She believed she was even having fun.

She made it to the diner where she was supposed to meet the CIA agent. She didn't want to meet any CIA agents. She didn't want to be at a diner in a giant cornfield. She didn't want her life to be changed so radically. She got out of her car, looked around and saw empty fields stretching for miles. She realized that she had never been to a place like this. There were people wearing overalls and cowboy hats. There were pickup trucks with rebel flag stickers on the windows. She walked into the diner. The diner looked old and sad. The servers were overweight women who had spent their lives in these fields, underneath giant skies and pounding rain storms, with amazing sunrises and sunsets.

She saw a man wearing a cowboy hat. It was true. Nevitsky had not lied. There he was, the CIA agent.

The CIA agent had been in the CIA since his early twenties. He went to college at Yale and got his master's there. He knew three languages: English, Spanish and Arabic. He had worked many twelve to fifteen hour days for the agency. At the beginning it felt like a beautiful dream come true. He was a CIA agent, something unique and special and awesome in American society. It was tantamount to being a movie star or the CEO of a Fortune 500 company. But instead of having fame or money he had secrets and the ability to wiretap people and sneak around the planet doing whatever he liked. He got to work in Iraq, Egypt, Peru and Colombia. He had lived his childhood dream of being a CIA agent, of seeing the world, of protecting his country. But one day he became bored with it. He didn't know why he was protecting America. The depression got worse and he didn't even know why he made a sandwich to eat it. Most of the time he would vomit the food he ate. He would eat a bowl of soup and vomit it up ten minutes later. He would get food from McDonald's and vomit. He decided to buy organic food from Whole Foods but he was still vomiting. He couldn't keep any sort of food down. He bought an I.V. and started running nutrients through a tube into his veins. He was in his mid-forties and had never married or had children. He had a big house but no one lived in it but him. He couldn't even get a cat because he spent so little time at home. He started to think, sometimes before he went to sleep, that the cause of his depression was all the traveling. He had gazed upon the pyramids of Egypt, upon Saint Sofia in Istanbul, upon the castle ruins of Europe, the Wailing Wall of Jerusalem, and he even made it to the Great Wall of China and the Forbidden City. He would look at those structures and be amazed by their beauty and how they were once built by great empires, full of vigor and strength. He imagined himself to not only be CIA but one of David's Mighty Men, a Janissary, a Samurai, a Praetorian Guard or a Persian Immortal. Sometimes the CIA agent would think, "Who were these people, these Janissaries? Weren't they just deluded men who defended their leaders blindly, without reason, just because they thought it was their duty, no other reason?" He started to wonder if he had any reason to defend the government, the free world, he started to wonder what the phrase 'free world' even meant. He started to question language and when one starts questioning language, everything they know becomes corrupt. He started to feel like America was just another predictable empire. They got their chance after the Second World War to become an empire and took it. They didn't even question it. They built a giant military, created the CIA, and they were off, never looking back. But what was the point of becoming an empire? To create peace, to protect your self-interests, to bring your ideology to the world whether the world wanted it or not? He felt predictable, even trite, that he was part of a government and culture that got sucked into the empire trap so easily. He realized this while sitting at a table drinking tea in Cairo. He went to work every day and said nothing about his feelings. He didn't know what to do with his life. He didn't know how to do anything else but be a CIA agent. What else could he do? Go work for a local police department and be bored out of his mind. He'd had offers to go into various lines of business, but that all seemed boring too. He decided to put his skills to a different use: espionage of his own government.

Monica walked over to the table and touched the seat and said, "May I sit?"

The man with the cowboy hat said, "Yeah, go ahead."

Monica looked at him. He was in his mid-forties, handsome, wore a nice long-sleeved, button-down shirt, blue jeans and cowboy boots. In her life she had never had a conversation with a CIA agent or with a man wearing a cowboy hat. It all made her nervous, the cornfield, the sad-looking people, the CIA agent. None of it made any sense to her. It all seemed absurd, but she wanted to find Michael and would do what was required of her.

The man said, "You are Monica Whitten. I have read your documents. You're a state university grad in computer science, you got above average grades. You grew up middle-class. You have lived basically a normal life. Is this true?"

"Yes, but who are you?"

"That isn't important."

"But why are you helping me?"

"I am helping because there was another committee and I disagreed with what they said, a committee just like the one Dr. Charles Nevitsky was part of, but this committee was different. Its goal wasn't to make America strong or to defeat the Soviets. The CIA did not invite great minds from all over America to participate. The committee was a bunch of stooge politicians and corporate assholes. The question was: how does America compete in the twenty-first century in a global economy with so much cheap labor in other countries? Their answer was that America needed a large amount of unemployed people which would lead to everyone's value being cheapened. We had to turn America into the third world to compete. Many protested and said there were real problems, global warming, the fact that the wealthy are buying up everything. No one cared. I have determined that no one cares, but I care. And I do not care where it leads us as long as someone does show some concern. So I will help you."

Monica didn't understand any of this. Why would her government join up with corporations to make life worse? Why would anyone want to make life worse? Monica's main problem with the situation was that she had grown up around people who believed that people strived to make their own lives better while at the same time showing a great deal of concern for the lives of others. Her father worked not only to make sure they got what they wanted but also to make sure she got what she wanted. She remembered times when her father would help his brother out with money. She remembered how her dad would shovel the older people's driveways in the neighborhood. She remembered how on holidays they would go to church and feed the poor. She remembered simple things like canned food drives she had done at high school. She thought about Michael and how he lived with his grandpa, helping the old man with daily chores he could no longer do. She recalled Hurricane Katrina and how she donated money to it and how she helped raise money for the people of Haiti when the earthquake happened. Monica's world was a world where people helped each other, where people shared and tried their best not to be selfish. The idea of people intentionally being selfish scared her. It confused her. She just didn't understand why a human would want to be selfish.

The man in the cowboy hat said, "I will help you find Michael." He pulled out a laptop and put it on the table. He showed her a satellite map. He pointed at a small little dot in the map and said, "This is Nevada. You need to go here." He pointed with his index finger and said, "This is where the camp is, fifty miles off any known highway. There is a dirt road that goes to it but you can't use that one, because you will be spotted. You need to park your car here and walk." He pointed at a little gas station, then he said, "Leave the keys in your car. Someone will pick it up."

Monica responded, "But that's my car."

"You won't need your car after that. Listen, what you know is over. Your old life is over. You will need to walk through the desert for two days. This will be very hard, but I will supply you with all you need. After you find the camp, you need to find Sherwood Burke." The man made the screen focus on the camp. He pointed with his index at a part of the fence and said, "At three in the morning Sherwood Burke will be standing at this point in the fence. You will give him the materials I will give you, then he will tell you what will happen."

Monica said in surprise, "Sherwood Burke, that crazy criminal from NEOTAP?"

"Sherwood Burke is a total and complete soldier. I would even say a warrior, a true leader and warrior. He shows no fear, no matter how loud and vicious the battle becomes. He remains calm, he remains at peace. He only feels alive when engaged in struggle and violence. He is my man on the inside."

"Do you know if Michael is okay?"

"Yes, Sherwood said he is fine. They have become friends."

Monica and the man finished their coffees and went outside. The cornfield and giant sky terrified Monica, but she was starting to come to terms with it. She had a direction now, a point at which to move. She could finally move with purpose and confidence.

They walked over to the man's truck. He pulled out a bag and showed Monica what was in it.

The man went over the supplies. Two bottles of water,

a small pillow, a sleeping bag, and a small amount of food. He said, "These are yours. It won't be hot so you won't need much water. Conserve your water. Snack a little bit every three hours but don't eat a lot at once." Then he took out a small handheld GPS system and night vision binoculars and said, "You will need to find the camp and locate where you should be." Then he pulled out five handguns, extra bullets and five grenades, and said, "Give these to Sherwood."

"I don't understand. Am I getting Michael out or starting a war?"

"You can't just get one person out. Either you get them all out or no one gets out. There will be a firefight, but there are over one-thousand prisoners and only sixty people on the staff. Half of the staff is cooks, janitors and case managers. There are five guard towers with high-powered machine guns that must be taken out." Then he pulled out bolt cutters and attached them to the backpack and said, "These are to cut the fence with."

"What the fuck is this shit? All I want is Michael, I can't be getting shot at by high-powered machine guns."

"You have to."

"Have to do what?"

"Get shot at or you won't get Michael back, or the men and the women in the camp won't be set free."

"I just want Michael."

"No, you want all of them because they are all Michael. Every single one of them is Michael. They are all a person trapped in that camp because of what they were thinking."

"What kind of fucking camp is this?" Monica said.

"A camp for those who think differently. Imagine NEO-TAP times a thousand. All day long they must attend classes, listen to speeches on responsibility, on the Five Pillars."

Monica stood there. She didn't know what to think. "But why me? I'm just some random IT girl."

The man looked at her and said, "Because you have to."

"How am I supposed to defeat people with high-powered machine guns?"

"Because they are idiots. Just use your intelligence. The people in charge now have been selected because they are afraid of thinking. Just outthink them."

He got in his truck and drove away. He didn't look back. He didn't wave. It was over. He had other things to do.

Monica stood there in front of the diner, amongst the cornfields. She took the supply bag and put it into her car and drove to the gas station where the CIA agent told her to abandon her car.

The Email Via Cellphone

Monica lay on a bed in a boring-looking hotel room. There was one picture on the wall. It was a cowboy riding a horse through the desert. She looked at the picture and thought, "Am I a cowboy?" She remembered watching cowboy movies with her dad when she was young. She never understood why her dad wanted to watch a bunch of white guys shoot each other in the desert. But she started to understand it was about adventure. She kept thinking about her dad and Michael.

She went to the bathroom and showered. She knew she needed to get nice and clean before walking through the desert. She lay on the bed and took another Xanax. The Xanax felt good. It felt like a soft waterfall, cool water pouring down on her. A soft breeze on a hot, humid day. She wanted to feel peaceful. It was hard though. She couldn't stop worrying. It was like life was relentless with responsibility. She fell asleep watching television. The television stayed on all night while she slept.

When she awoke in the morning she brushed her teeth and made a small pot of coffee. She put her clothes on and noticed a small envelope under the door. Monica felt panic and picked it up, walked over to the bed and sat down. She opened the letter carefully and unfolded the pages. The words were typed neatly in Helvetica. On the top of the letter, written in pen: "From Ashley/keep going"

The letter was from Mike, apparently typed up on a cellphone and sent as an email to Ashley, who printed it out and delivered it to Monica:

monica
it is michael
ive disappeared
i was able to write you this email because burke had a cellphone smuggled in the camp where im staying
this is what happened
i got to work
standing there drinking latte from starbucks
berg comes up to me says michael, come with me to office
didnt want to go to office
wnted to tell her to fuck herself
shld have
shld have ran out of the building
didnt
went to office with berg
she told me to sit down
sat down
she sat down
both sitting
she asked if i wanted soda to drink said okay
berg left office
got soda

gave it to me

drank it

started 2 feel weird

last memory seeing berg sitting there with stone cold
facial expression

berg face no humanity no life nothing

passed out

woke up in airplane

looked

fucking insane

was on an airplane

panic

knew something was wrong

saw two men in their 20s dressed in military fatigues

machine guns

was cuffed 2 chair

knew i was fucked

knew i had disappeared

been arrested

thought

this must be a mistake

is this a joke

why would the govt arrest me

im boring

i go to work

go home

do nothing with my life

drive the speed limit

im boring

person that plays by rules

what rule did i break

couldnt think of 1 law i broke to get stuck in an airplane

and guarded by men with machine guns

why would they need machine guns

fucking machine guns

machine guns are scary monica

never been violent in my life

insane

didnt understand reasoning behind arrest and machine
guns

knew it was horrible

that i was fucked

didnt say anything at first

pretended was passed out

listened 2 soldiers talk hoping would hear something
that would help me

soldiers kept talking abt their wives kids

1 soldier was excited his kid was starting to walk

drove him nuts that his kid ws putting everything in his
mouth

other soldier told him he had a 7 y/o

said his kid would get over that stage

move on to do other strange crazy things

they both laughed

they talked about their kids like they really loved them

nothing said about where we were going or my situation

decided to wake

ask them a question hey

they looked at me

said why am i on this plane should be at work

soldier with 7 y/o we can't help you

but what are you doing now

we are guarding you

you don't know why im here

soldier tired of hearing me speak said
we arent the people that can help you we have orders
what about my rights
soldier said
please be quiet
sat quiet
machine guns make a person quiet
they couldnt help me
they had orders
after an hour the plane landed
soldiers uncuffed me from the seat
took me off the plane
looked around
it was the desert
but what desert
it could be any desert
could be sahara or gobi
asked soldiers where am i
soldier with child learning to walk in a desert
he laughed
he didnt care about me
it was hard to be around humans that cared so little
about me
they cared nothing about giving me attention or anything i wanted
they had no desire to fulfill any of my needs
they led me to a large compound
was terrified
wanted to fall on the ground
cry
knew that wasnt an option
it would have made things worse
saw machine gunners posted on towers

saw people that werent dressed in military fatigues
realized this is where people went when they disappeared
led me in compound
compound here is new very clean
led me into a room
had me sit on a plastic chair at round table
soldiers left
locked the door behind them
sat there staring into space
left me nothing to read
not even a magazine
put my head on arms
went to sleep
hours passed
no one came to speak to me
tried lying on floor
soldier came in room
told me to get back in chair
got back chair
more hours passed
must have been in chair 20 hrs
woman came in wearing nice military clothes
not fatigues
class As
think they are called
was a white woman in her 30s
slightly overweight
she said my name is mrs techak i am your case worker
how are you doing today michael
want to know why im here
im not the person to speak to for that techak very polite
voice

who is

im not the person to speak to for that she took out few pieces of paper put them in front of me said could you please answer these questions

i dont understand am i under arrest

this is a treatment center michael

didnt check myself into a treatment center this doesn't look like a treatment center

why are you being nasty we are trying to help you said techak

looks like i am under arrest and detained

could you please fill out the papers

she left the room

looked at paper

it was a questionnaire

questions were stupid

they asked me

are you being treated well at the camp

was my plane ride comfortable

were the soldiers nice to me

did the sleeping agent they gave me work properly

were there any side effects such as diarrhea incontinence impotence

was the plastic chair i was sitting on comfortable

had to answer from 1 to 5 strongly disagree to strongly agree

it was insane

answered questions out of boredom

least i could read something

sat there for 3 more hours

no sound in the room except a heater that would pump in dry stale air no music

no sounds of outside world

nothing

couldnt even hear people walking in hall

dismal

could feel my mind lose itself from lack of sleep

and lack of sound

techak came back

she sat down

picked up questionnaire

put it in her bag

said are you going to tell me why ive been arrested now

she stared at me said first off welcome to lupejanko treatment center

pronounced lupejanko with spanish accent loo pay yanko

please just tell me why ive been arrested

you haven't been arrested you have been scheduled to enter this treatment center because of your behavior

what am i guilty of

what do you think you are guilty of

dont think im guilty of anything ive always considered myself boring

she looked at me said that is what they all say everyone says they are innocent therefore if everyone says they are innocent everyone must be guilty

that doesnt make any sense

we have your behaviors here we know your behaviors

are you an interrogator you look like an interrogator

im a case manager not an interrogator

am i guilty of being a witch

she gave me a look of disapproval

okay you got me im a witch i practice black magic

shut up

okay

you need to take this serious

sat there feeling shitty

there didn't seem any hope that anything i said mattered

terrible feeling of oppression struck me

started to hyperventilate but sucked it back

i was going to vomit

realized that i was not the kind of person that could perform well during interrogation

just didn't know what to do

had no experience in the art of being interrogated

there was no hope

was trapped

like the residents of NEOTAP

techak said in a tone that was like an iron heel grinding my skull deep into the dirt of the earth you have done several things that are not responsible we have a list here first thing you did was not perform your job at NEOTAP with success you always told the residents why you were doing things you were told never to give the residents of NEOTAP reasons for your behavior or for the rules of NEOTAP but you did anyway you often let people get away with things because you viewed some of the rules as stupid in our opinion were not stupid

you are saying that i was too nice i allowed the residents to have their humanity

she said i do not approve of that reply

okay what else did i do

you subverted capitalism this year 3 times first you raked the leaves of a neighbors yard for free this neighbor was named mr brown then you shoveled the snow off mrs mays driveway twice for free even though she offered you money

mrs mays husband is a truck driver he wasnt going to be home til late at night she needed to get somewhere i shoveled her driveway i raked those leaves to take the leaves and use them as compost for my garden

yes we know you have a garden and the garden is organic so

what is wrong with tomatoes and peppers from the grocery store said techak.

they are full of fertilizers food at grocery stores is half natural gas they arent even food

why didnt you take money for shoveling that snow mr scipio

it seemed like the right thing to do

she looked with anger said what if everyone in our culture started doing the right thing

i don't know

our culture is based off self interest not self sacrifice the capitalist system requires self interested people to do things for money if everyone went around doing things for free the whole system would fall apart are you trying to destroy the economic system of america

dont think so

she said your crime is more heinous than stealing from a store or even selling drugs because if you steal from a store then you are still stating that you believe in capitalism you just cant afford to buy certain products if you sell drugs you are still selling them for money which is capitalism but your behavior doing things for free growing your own food these are terrible behaviors that subvert and slowly destroy the very foundation of our culture and country

i need a lawyer i need my rights to be protected

you arent under arrest mr scipio this is a treatment center

but you are detaining me there are people with machine guns here guarding me

you are in a treatment center you are being helped we will help you

you cant do this

i personally dont know what you are talking about

who can i talk to there must be somebody here that isnt insane this seems like a mistake how can someone be detained for shoveling somebodys driveway for free

she stood up left

sat in plastic chair for more hours

tired

feeling terrible

2 soldiers i never met before came in room

walked me to the open area where the prisoners were kept

they led me to a bed

threw down toothpaste toothbrush walked away

sat there on bed dejected

burke sat next to me

looked at him said are you mad at me about the piss test

he smiled said no

asked him who was in charge of the camp

he told me that no one was

everyone at the camp was just a person taking orders

he told me to go to sleep in the morning they were going to wake us all up to eat

then to go to class

they want to reform us because we are dangerous

didnt understand anything

lay down on the bed

passed out
woke up the next day to loud sirens
every morning we wake up to loud sirens
devastating
need to get out of here
dont know why im here
im not ready for the concentration camp lifestyle
dont know what is happening
burke says he has a plan
says youre coming that he has agents collecting intel
dont know what he is talking about
dont know what is going on
miss you
miss your body next to mine
miss you the funny things you say
miss your arms legs vagina
wish i would have never gotten that job at NEOTAP
wish everything was different
doesnt matter what i wish
this is the truth of the situation
i am in a prison that calls itself a treatment center
miss you
rescue me
i love you
michael

Monica finished the email. She felt a sense of calm because she at least knew Michael was alive. But she felt angrier than ever knowing that her man was stuck in some crazy treatment center in the middle of the desert. She packed up her things and headed toward the location the CIA agent told her about.

March into the Desert

Monica parked her car at the gas station in the Nevada desert. She had never been in the desert before. It all looked alien and strange. She stood outside her car. The sun blasted down on her, but it wasn't hot because it was the end of October. She looked bad. Her weave hadn't been combed in days. She hadn't showered or put on makeup. She thought about going home but she realized she was having too much fun. She remained steadfast in her resolve to find Michael even if that meant engaging in a giant firefight and dying.

She left the keys in the ignition and threw on the heavy backpack. She said out loud, "Oh my fucking god this is heavy." She didn't know how she was going to carry this backpack fifty miles, but she pulled out the GPS and started walking into the desert. Before long the gas station and the road were out of sight. She was nowhere. The comforts of civilization had disappeared. Monica realized that no one could see her, no one knew where she was. The only thing that could see her was God. She imagined God looking down from Heaven at her walking through the desert by herself carrying a fifty pound backpack. She imagined God looking down knowing that His creation was powerful. God had created plants that would fight to survive in any situation, that would evolve and change if need be, that God had birds that could fly thousands of miles and fish that could live at the bottom of the ocean, and volcanoes that could destroy whole civilizations, and He had also created a species that would fight and die and murder to get its version of justice. She understood then why God had let evil into the world, why evil existed, because it gave humans a chance to show their power and worth. Monica believed in a God that required people showing their worth. She felt alone before her God for the first time in her life. She felt that God could see that she was worthy of being a human, worthy in sharing His creation, worthy of being created at all.

Monica sat on a rock and took a small drink of water and said, "So this is it, God, just me and you. Do you think I can do this? You must."

Monica kept walking. Her feet started to blister, her legs became sore, her whole body started to feel extreme pain, but she kept walking. She had no intention of stopping.

She walked for a whole day and saw no one. The gun still sat under her coat, resting there in case she needed it.

When night came she unfolded her sleeping bag and sat on it and ate. She lit a small fire and warmed her hands. She took her shoes off, examined her blisters and rubbed her legs. In the backpack was a tube of Icy Hot. She took the tube out and rubbed the cream into her skin. She felt exhausted but couldn't fall asleep immediately. She could hear the sounds of night around her. She could even smell the night. She looked up at the stars and could see more stars than she had ever seen in her life. She was amazed by the beauty of the desert sky. She was scared but amazed. The desert night made her smile. She thought she needed to smile because it might be her last night alive and she needed to take it seriously. She wanted to solve this problem, the problem of being without Michael, the problem of all those people being trapped in that camp. She didn't understand the full complexity of the situation, how it stretched back to the fifties, how it involved high level officials in the government, corporations, and CIA agents, but she understood her place in the grand scheme of events. All life, all civilization, was every little human participating in their own little way, and she was just another little person doing her duty, doing what must be done. She said a prayer to the Christian God she had grown up with as she fell asleep. "I will carry this backpack, God, to Sherwood Burke. I will free those people."

The Final March

Monica woke up in the desert. She looked around and felt confused that she wasn't in her room. She remembered her room, waking up day after day to an alarm clock, getting up, showering, then going to work. But life became different. Now she woke up in the desert, in a huge alien landscape. She kept looking around at the mountains, at the strange plants, and sometimes she even saw a lizard or some jackrabbits. All of it excited her. She promised herself that if she lived through this, she would return to the desert and explore with Michael and take some good pictures.

She walked all day, stopping only a few times. When she would get tired, she would take an Adderall, drink water and eat a little. At times she grew angry and wanted to scream, at other times she wanted to cry. But she kept walking. Her body ached, her feet hurt, her legs didn't want to move, but she kept moving.

Monica wanted to stop and give up late in the afternoon but she refused. She didn't understand why it had to be her, why life had given her this situation. She felt cheated, but she would endure.

As night came on, the GPS said she only had two miles to go. She walked to the top of a small mountain as the sun receded over the horizon, took out her night vision binoculars and looked down on the camp. "There it is," she said.

She looked down on it. It was huge. Everyone was forced to sleep outside on bunk beds in open air pavilions. There was a large building where she assumed the military and employees slept. There were five guard towers. She could see the machine guns. They looked huge and terrifying. There was a tower on all four corners and a tower stationed on top of the building where the staff slept.

Still, she was alone. No one knew she was up there except the CIA agent and maybe Sherwood Burke, but even they couldn't be sure. It was possible to assume that she had died out in the desert. It was possible to assume she had given up.

She realized that the people down there in that camp were suffering just like her. They were forced to live in a sad prison in the middle of the desert. They were suffering like her. There were millions suffering like her. She was not alone. She felt strong. She felt that she had the power of God running through her. She didn't know what that meant, but she felt it.

She went to sleep and set her alarm for a few hours later. When she awoke, she would meet up with Sherwood and rescue Michael.

The Impossible

At one in the morning, Monica woke up and examined her body again. Her feet were covered in blisters and her legs could barely move. The pain was terrible, and the idea of running or even hurrying seemed impossible to her. She wanted to lie down for three days and watch movies on Netflix cuddling Michael, but that would never happen again unless she walked down to that camp and saved him.

She stood, grunting, and put on the heavy backpack. She winced and even cried a little the pain was so bad, but she kept moving. She put on the backpack and strapped it up. She made sure she knew where her extra bullets for the gun under her coat were. She made sure that she was ready.

Monica slowly walked down the mountain to the camp. Her mind and body were sore. She thought for a second that she wouldn't look very pretty for Michael, but she realized that Michael probably didn't look good either.

She looked at her GPS and figured out where she needed to be and at what time. She could see the fifteen foot high razor wire fence. There were giant lights but many of them were turned off. She walked to the dark spot in the fence the CIA agent had told her to approach. No one was there. She looked at her watch. It read 2:48AM. She realized she was early. She was always early. It was a long twelve minutes. She kept thinking she would die, that the men in the towers would see her and shoot her. She would be dead and not even get to see Michael. Then Sherwood Burke and Michael arrived at the fence. Monica smiled, as did Michael. He touched the fence. Monica reached out and touched his hand. Their hands touched. It felt so good to both of them, so sweet, so tender, so like a miracle.

Michael said, "I love you so much."

"I love you so much also," Monica said.

"Okay, that's enough," Sherwood Burke said. "You will have time to fuck and suck later, no fucking and sucking now. Monica, where are the bolt cutters?"

"I have them here." She detached them from the bag and said, "Here they are."

Sherwood Burke said, "Cut a hole in the fence and give me the bag."

"Okay."

Monica slowly cut a hole in the fence. While she cut, Michael told her how all they did all day was attend classes where they talked about responsibility and how to follow procedure properly. Monica asked him if they fed him well, Michael said they made him eat shitty American food every day. Boiled steaks and hamburgers, mac and cheese and Snicker bars. It was disgusting.

Monica finished cutting the hole and handed the bag through. "Can we leave now?"

Sherwood Burke said, "No, by ourselves we can't leave. They will catch us. We have to take over, we have to fight. There is no running anymore. The plan is already set into motion. I have separated everyone into three groups: the Seminoles, Apaches and Comanches. The Seminoles will attack the four surrounding towers, the Apaches will attack the doors of the base, and the Comanches will take the tower located on top of the main building." Sherwood Burke opened the backpack and took out the guns and grenades and said, "Three of the guns will go to Apaches who will attack the base. I will take two of the guns and attack the towers. The grenades will be divided up between the Apaches and Comanches. This is going to turn into one hell of a firefight. A lot of people might get scared and just hide even though they said they would fight. This is to be expected. But we have them grossly outnumbered. Even if six-hundred of us don't back down, we should win. We also realized that a certain part of the beds can be detached to make spears."

"Fuck spears. They have machine guns," Monica said.

"All the Zulus had were spears and they beat the British a couple of times," Sherwood Burke said, laughing.

All three of them snuck back into the area where the bunks were. Everyone was awake and ready, just pretending to sleep. Sherwood handed out the guns and grenades. Monica looked around. Nobody looked happy about what was happening. Everyone looked scared. But they were ready. Everyone got out of bed and detached the homemade spears from their bunk beds.

Monica sat down on a bed next to Michael. Monica said to Sherwood, "I read your Talking Points. Is that really enough to start a full-scale revolution? I mean, do you have any other justification for this, any ideology? I want to know why I might die tonight."

"Because they have decided to point guns at us, they

have decided to break the laws of this land for the sake of their own comfort and pride."

"I know that, I know they are pointing guns at us, I know they are breaking laws, I know what they are doing is unjust, but what makes what we are doing just?" Monica had become stronger over the course of the last several days. She had learned she had more courage and determination than she ever thought she had.

"Because I don't believe Locke's interpretation of the Bible and private ownership was accurate. Locke's interpretation leads mankind to destroy the environment, but I don't believe the Bible states that."

"Then what is your proof," Monica said.

Burke sat on a bed and picked up a Bible and said, "They let you have Bibles here, the only book they will allow. Prisons never change." He opened the Bible. "Locke used Psalm 115:16 to justify private ownership and the destruction of the planet, 'The heavens are the Lord's heavens but the earth he has given to human beings.' That is Locke's verse, which is in the Old Testament, but the verse that comes from the New Testament stating who owns the earth is from Colossians 1:15. 'He is the image of the invisible God, the firstborn of all creation; for in him all things in heaven and on earth were created, things visible and invisible, whether thrones or dominions or rulers or powers – all things have been created through him and for him.' That verse obviously states that the earth was created for Christ, therefore if everything was created for Christ we must treat everything with empathy and love."

Monica said, "I don't know if your logic works. It just means that everything is for Jesus. It doesn't explain what it means."

"But obviously Locke used selective reading. He specifically selected a verse that was good for his wants and needs, just as I am using a verse picked specifically for my wants and needs. It's all just interpretation. We need to give people a new interpretation of looking at nature. The Bible is the way to do that. I also found a verse in the Qur'an from the House of 'Imran 3:109: 'To God belongs all that is in the heavens and on earth.' Christianity and Islam agree that the earth belongs to God, so we should protect it and treat it with love."

Mike said, "What about the Jews and Asians who don't care about Christianity and Islam?"

Burke laughed. "The Asians have capitalism now. They have private ownership, and they have never asked where it came from. They don't care at all that their economic systems are based off an old Jewish poem."

"This really makes mankind look stupid," Monica said.

"Yes, they truly are fucking stupid. But I have one more verse, Revelation 11:18. 'The nations raged/but your wrath has come/and the time for judging the dead/for rewarding your servants/the prophets, and saints and all who fear your name/both small and great/and for destroying those who destroy the earth.'" Burke paused, smiled and said, "'I am the destroyer of those who destroy the earth.'"

"Isn't that a poem?" Michael said.

Burke smiled. "Yes."

"This is insane," Monica said.

Burke stood and in a few quick movements grabbed Monica by the back of her hair, pulled her to her feet, dragged her over to look at the towers with the machine gunners. He moved her body like it was nothing, Monica could feel Burke's strength, his immense energy and determination. It

173

scared her. Burke said in the most vicious voice Monica had ever heard, "Look at those towers. Look at them, Monica. You see that? This is war! They have taken Michael and I, stolen us without telling anyone, without trial, without reading us our rights, they drugged us and put us here in this shithole in the middle of the desert, they have broken their own laws for the sake of their own comfort and pride, they feel so entitled to what they have they are willing to put their own citizens in unknown locations without any contact with their family and friends, they point guns at us every day. That is war, Monica. This is war. Making friends and compromise aren't possible anymore. We can't vote our way out of this mess. The only thing left is absolute and total war with the enemy. They have left us no choice."

Monica felt his strong hand squeezing her hair. She felt the hair ripping out of her scalp. She felt terrified in the presence of Sherwood Burke. She knew he could kill her, that if she needed to be exterminated for the cause, he could make it happen.

Burke said, "Don't you understand, to beat them we have to be worse than them. It is Newton's First Law. The velocity of a body remains constant unless it is acted upon by an external force. We must be stronger than their force to stop them. We must stop their velocity."

"Yes, I understand," Monica said.

Burke let Monica go and went back to getting the guns prepared.

Mike sat there. He did nothing to help Monica, but unlike Monica he had been in the camp for several days and knew that Burke was his only hope. Mike didn't have the physical prowess or communication to convince Monica how bad the situation was, so he let Burke do it.

Before Burke decided to start the battle, he shouted a prayer from Psalm 68:

"Let God Arise!

His enemies shall be scattered!

Let those who hate the Lord flee!

As smoke is driven away

Drive them away!

As wax melts before fire!

The wicked shall die at the presence of God!

Let the righteous be glad;

Let them rejoice before God!

A father of the fatherless, a defender of widows,

Is God in his holy habitation.

He frees those who are bound in slavery!

And leaves the rebellious to die on sun scorched earth!

God will crush the heads of his enemies!

The hairy scalp of the ones who profit through sins!

The Lord said, 'I will bring them back from Bashan.

I will bring them back from the depths of the sea!

So your foot may crush them in blood!

And the mouths of dogs may chew upon your enemies!'"

Sherwood Burke screamed the last line. Then he told everyone to prepare for war. The crowd of detained prisoners charged out from the shelter. Through a loudspeaker, a guard in a tower said, "Get back in your bunks, go to sleep! Sit down, go back to your bunks and lie down."

Monica stood next to Michael, holding his hand. She said, "Do you think Sherwood is the Wrath of God?"

"I believe him to be extraordinary, and he makes me

want to be," Michael said.

Monica and Michael kissed. Monica looked up at the sky and said, "The stars are pretty in the desert."

"Yes, they are nice."

Sherwood screamed at the guard in the tower, "Suck my fucking dick!" Then Sherwood raised a handgun and fired.

The Seminoles sprinted at the four surrounding towers. The five machine guns started blasting into the crowds. Body parts were flying. Blood was shot into the air. The sound of human screams. The Apaches attacked the doors of the base and the Comanches started trying to get on top of the building.

The machine guns were firing. The noise was horrible. No one could hear what anyone else was saying. Among the sounds of the machine guns were the wails of wounded humans, screaming in agony.

Sherwood Burke ran at high speeds with his guns hidden. He knew the men in the towers would be more focused on the people trying to capture them. He knew this and did not tell the Seminoles. He ran outside the waves of the crowds, looking more like an innocent, scared idiot than a revolutionary leader. He had marked out where the perfect shot would be and got to the first one quickly. He pulled out his gun and fired and hit the first man in the tower. The young guard was shot in the head. The bullet pierced his brain. He fell beside the machine gun. The Seminoles took the tower, crawled into the machine gunner's box and began firing at the tower on top of the building. The taking of the first gun gave courage to the rest. Cheers and screams were heard. The sound was immense under the desert stars.

Sherwood Burke then raced amongst the dead and screaming bodies, looking down and seeing his fellow humans ripped into shreds around him. He ran on. He had seen this in Iraq. He was used to it.

The soldiers came pouring out of the barracks, still sleepy-eyed, but armed with machine guns. They began firing into the crowd. The three men with the handguns shot at them until their bullets ran out. The prisoners with the spears ran in. The soldiers unloaded on whoever looked like a prisoner.

Michael and Monica sprinted at one of the towers holding spears, screaming at the top of their lungs, although they had lost all sense of fear. They knew they had to win or they would die there. When Monica saw a soldier leave the building she took the gun from her holster, cocked it and fired. She hit the soldier in the shoulder. He fell to the ground, screaming. Other prisoners pounced on him and stabbed him with spears.

Sherwood Burke took out another tower. The screams were horrible now. The sounds of bullets being fired was horrible. If God was watching, he was seeing the best and worst of humanity.

Then bullets finally took down Monica and Michael. One went through Michael's stomach and he fell to the ground screaming. Another bullet pierced Monica's lung. She lay there trying to talk, trying to breath, but nothing. She knew that she was going to die. Michael looked at her and crawled toward her, his guts dragging in the sand, scraping on rocks as he crawled. He made it over to Monica, cradled her in his arms. Her body twitched in his arms. It took everything he had but he spooned her like they were just going to sleep for the night. He put his arm around her and said into her ear, "Let's watch a movie on Netflix," and they both died.

The firefight raged on. Sherwood Burke went from tower to tower shooting out the guards until there were none left. The remaining soldiers and staff inside the prison threw down their guns because they knew they were outnumbered.

After the battle was over, Sherwood Burke walked over to the spot where Monica and Michael lay dead. He went down on one knee and said in a sad voice, "The cruelty of politics," and then stood and walked away.

He walked in front of everyone and said, "I am now Sherwood Kahn!" Everyone screamed in jubilation. The prisoners believed in him for he was a commander who had slept and fought with his soldiers.

Sherwood Burke walked out into the desert. The sun slowly rose in the east. Burke looked around and felt a sense of beauty. He smiled and felt happy about what he had done and what he was planning to do. He finally felt that he was in control. He wasn't just a pawn for other people. He walked further out into the desert to a mountaintop where Ashley sat with a camera aimed at the violence that just took place. Ashley had been live streaming the battle online.

"Did it work?" Sherwood Burke asked.

"Yes," Ashley said.

"It's a beautiful morning, isn't it?"

"Yes."

Ashley sat there smiling.

"The world is a sad, strange place," Sherwood Burke said.

"Yes, it is."

Go to work and do your job.
Care for your children.
Pay your bills.
Obey the law.
Buy products.

ABOUT THE AUTHOR

Noah Cicero grew up in Youngstown, Ohio and later moved to South Korea. He's living in Las Vegas for now. *The Collected Works of Noah Cicero Vol. I*, a collection of his early novels and short stories, is also available from Lazy Fascist Press.

CPSIA information can be obtained at www.ICGtesting.com
Printed in the USA
LVOW06s2224160114

369813LV00005B/309/P